The Stone Wall Crossing

The Stone Wall Crossing

Abby Whittier's Journey Through Time

Alice Schellhorn Magrane

ISBN: 0692946764
ISBN 13: 9780692946763

CONTENTS

"Do you think the universe fights for souls to be together? Some things are too strange and strong to be coincidences."

-Emery Allen

PROLOGUE

I 've waited more than a year to write down the details of what I experienced. I knew I had to write it down now, in this journal, or I might forget important details if I waited any longer. Events do get hazy as they fade in your memory. I was torn between writing this story or just pretending it never happened because I know once it's written, people who eventually read it and don't know me might think I was some sort of crazy person.

But I can assure you that the people who do know me—my parents, friends and teachers—know I'm someone who's absolutely not prone to living in a fantasy world. I live in the here and now, which makes this story even more unbelievable. But it happened, exactly as I'm writing it down on these pages. I have no explanation for what happened to me. I only know that it did. I'm keeping this record and maybe, someday, I'll decide to let others read it too. For now it's enough to just get it on paper so I won't forget the most amazing experience of my life.

CHAPTER 1

THE MOVE

New England. As far back as I can remember, I'd hear my parents talk about New England. I didn't know what those words would mean to my life—or maybe I should say, to my lives.

I was growing up in Nevada where my dad worked for Atlas, one of the world's biggest casino and entertainment corporations. He didn't run the casinos or anything like that. As I grew up, I figured out that he was involved in the expansion of the casino business. He was like an executive in the company who looked at places where there were no casinos and tried to figure out how to get those places to allow them. I'm sure there was more to it than that, but that's all I needed to know, really.

My parents had both grown up in Massachusetts, one of the states in New England, and that's why I used to hear them, late at night, talking about how maybe someday, they could possibly move back there. But I was busy with school, taking lots of hard classes, belonging to a lot of clubs, and playing sports. So I didn't pay much attention to their late-night chats until I had no choice.

I arrived home from school late one afternoon to our Las Vegas townhouse. Our home was a really beautiful townhouse in the Summerlin area, high on a hill overlooking the Las Vegas strip. If you stood out on our deck at night, you could see the brilliant lights of the Strip illuminating the sky. I really loved to do that! My mom was waiting for me with an air of excitement that I don't remember ever seeing her display before.

"Abby," she asked, "can you sit for a minute before you start your homework? I really need to talk to you."

And then I got the news: we were moving back to my parents' home state. Massachusetts. New England. I knew where that was on a map of the U.S., but all it meant to me was leaving my friends, my school, my beautiful home in the desert, and the fun times I had always associated with living in Las Vegas.

Everything I had read about Massachusetts, and New England in general, made me believe I would hate it. Hate. It. They had awful winters with big blizzards. It rained a lot, and everyone was always harping on history. I have to say that my worst subject was history. I thought it was so boring. What counts is now. I just sat there and looked at my Mom, who was obviously very happy about this move, and I couldn't even find the words to tell her how awful I felt.

"I'm going up to my room," was all I could say as I ran up the stairs.

It was early April of my sophomore year at Palm Desert High and I had been hoping to make the varsity soccer team next fall. No tryouts for me. No ski club, no student council, no junior prom—I'd be leaving it all behind. I buried my head in my pillow and cried. Then I called my best friend, Julie. Julie Sanders and I had grown up together and were like sisters, maybe because both of us were only children. I was crying when she answered the phone.

"Jules," I sobbed, "I'm moving!"

"What's the problem?" she asked. "Did your parents buy a new house?"

"You don't understand," I wailed, "we're moving to Massachusetts, to the East Coast. We'll never see each other again."

"Oh my God! That's so awful! Can you come over so we can talk some more?"

"Meet me at the swings," I begged.

Whenever we wanted to talk and not be overheard by anyone, we always went to the swings at our old elementary school. Although they were usually full of kids in the hours just after school, by suppertime they were basically deserted. I stole out the back door, sneaking a peek at my mom, hoping she wouldn't see me. But her back was turned and she was on the phone, deep in conversation, probably about the move—right? I waited for Julie, and when she arrived, we just hugged and cried. Being the emotional one, I just couldn't wrap my head around the fact that I'd be leaving the place where I'd spent my whole life, and I'd have to start all over again in a place I knew I'd hate. Julie was always the more practical one. After we had both cried for a bit, she sniffled, blew her nose, and just as she had always done, she started making plans.

"Okay, Abby, we can FaceTime every night. And you can post photos of your new friends on Instagram so I know who you're talking about. And then I can come and visit you on school vacation in January. You'll meet new people and probably be really popular. After all, you **are** from Vegas! This might even be exciting!"

It's not that I didn't believe her. I wanted to. But trying to imagine myself in a whole different part of the country, in a new high school, just made me cry harder. When I was finally cried out, I hugged Julie again.

"I should probably go home and learn more about us moving," I moaned. "I don't even know when it's happening."

We both went off in different directions, as I walked slowly down the path leading to our condo development, and Julie walked towards hers. I walked into the house and ran smack into my mom, who was obviously waiting for me.

"Where were you?"

"I was down at High Ridge Elementary with Julie."

"Abby, we have to talk after dinner. I'm sorry this news upset you so much. I sort of knew you would hate the idea of moving, but it's critical to dad's career and we really have no choice."

"It's fine for you," I cried. "You've always wanted to move back to Massachusetts. Now you have your big chance. This isn't fair for me at all. I'm the one who has to leave everything I love and all my friends to go to some awful, cold part of the country where I'll have to start all over again!"

"Honey, I know. I know. I would have felt the same way when I was your age. Come and have some dinner and we can talk about it more."

That was it for me. Dinner? I didn't think so.

"I don't feel like eating at all now. Thanks a lot!" I called as I ran back up to my room and slammed the door. I just sat for awhile, thinking about what my life would possibly be like in a new town, in a new high school, with no friends. It was really going to suck.

Somehow, I got through the rest of the school year. I honestly don't know how I held it together. Every day as I walked to my classes with my friends, or went shopping at the mall, or did anything at all, I kept thinking, "This is one of the last times I'll be doing this." I thought my guidance counselor, Mrs. Green, might help figure out how to stop me from feeling this awful sense of doom, so I made an appointment to see her. She sympathized with me and told me that she'd contact the guidance department at my new school once I knew where I'd be living, but in the end, there was nothing she could really do about the move. At least she knew how I felt and wished I didn't have to go through it.

Meanwhile, my parents made a trip to Massachusetts over Memorial Day weekend to scope out places to live. I stayed over at Julie's, even though I could have gone with my parents. What difference would it make if I went? I'd rather spend some of the time I had left with my best friend, not house hunting, for God's sake!

When my parents returned from that trip, they told me they had bought a home in a small city, Haverhill, not too far from Boston. Haverhill. God, even the names of things out there sounded old-fashioned! They showed me pictures of the house. It was as different from our townhome in Las Vegas as it could possibly be. I was used to modern-type homes with stucco walls, lots of tile, glass and stone, and red terra cotta roofs. That's what they build out here in the desert. This house looked like something out of a storybook.

"It's a colonial," my dad explained.

The colonial was two stories, straight up and down, with a three-car garage attached to the house, and it had a basement. No one has a basement in Las Vegas. All the windows were rectangular, and everything was "square." At least that's how I would describe it. It was a pale grey color, with white shutters, and the door was the color of cinnamon. My dad told me it was in a beautiful development called Northwoods that had lots of woods and trees, as well as a golf course, a swimming pool and clubhouse. I have to admit, it sounded nice.

"How many months of the year do they even have summer up there?" I asked. (I actually never thought people in those New England states would have pools because the summers would be too cold.)

"The pool opens on Memorial Day and closes the weekend after Labor Day in September," my dad explained.

And so it was done. Our townhouse sold in two weeks. The company paid for movers to come and pack up everything—all of our furniture, cars, and clothes—and move it across the country. I had already said my goodbyes to my friends and promised to FaceTime as much as I could. Julie and I had one last sleepover, and on July 1, we flew from McCarren Airport in Las Vegas where there were slot machines everywhere, to Logan Airport in Boston where I saw signs for lobster and seafood chowder and Dunkin' Donuts from the moment I stepped into the terminal. I felt like I had landed on another planet.

CHAPTER 2

WHO AM I?

I guess I was so upset about the move, that I never really introduced myself at the beginning of my story. (Sometimes I get ahead of myself!) I'm Abigail Whittier, but as you've already figured out, absolutely everyone calls me Abby. In fact, I don't ever remember being called Abigail, except when teachers do roll call at the beginning of each school year. I can't really tell you what I look like, except that I have my mother's naturally blond hair that I wear long, so I don't have to take ages styling it. I got my brown eyes from my dad, and I guess it's from his side of the family that my tiny build comes from because my Granny Whittier is one of the tiniest people I've ever known. But I'm pretty strong, even though I'm small, and I love to play sports of every kind, as you've probably guessed.

My mom is Elizabeth Duston Whittier. I guess you'd have to say that she's pretty glamorous compared to other mothers, but she has to be. With my dad in the casino management business here in Las Vegas, she's always had to dress up and go with him to all kinds of functions and nightclubs. And the day after, in the RJ (that's the *Las Vegas Review Journal*), I usually see her photo, looking awesome, next to some famous person. But at home, she's just "Mom," and even though she usually wears jeans and jerseys, she always looks amazing!

There's not a lot to say about my dad, Jared Whittier, except he's really tall and good-looking in a male model kind of way. He's thirty-nine now and just starting to go a tiny bit grey, which he hates, but I think it makes him look distinguished and so does my mom. Both of my parents are really into fitness, and they built a gym into one of the rooms in our house so they could work out without having to join a gym. I love the equipment and use it on a pretty regular basis too.

I probably should also explain that I really do love my parents. I have always been close to them, and since I was their only child, they had always tried to give me the things I wanted and needed. We went on lots of short vacation trips together, and I always considered them much more fun than my friends' parents. Even though I got good grades in school, it was never because they put pressure on me. I guess that up until this move, our life had been as good as anyone's could be. I knew they were worried about me. I could tell by the way they looked at me and then, when they thought I wasn't looking, they looked at each other with a worried kind of look. My dad wasn't around much that summer. He was working long hours, trying to put together a proposal that would win his company the right to build a casino in Massachusetts. So my mom and I would go to the pool and relax, after working around the new house, opening boxes and deciding where to put things.

I'd never had a steady boyfriend at Palm Desert High and that was probably a good thing because it would have made moving even harder. Not that I didn't go out with guys. I always had a date to the proms and other school events, and I had lots of guys as my good friends, but I had never really been in a relationship. Believe it or not, that all changed when I moved. One of the first days my mom and I went to the pool, I dove in and was swimming laps. It felt so good that day. I guess I hadn't realized that there actually were days that reached 90 degrees in Massachusetts and they weren't like the dry, 90 degree days in Las Vegas. They were humid. I **did not like** humidity. The air was so thick you felt as though a warm, wet blanket was weighing down on you when you were outside.

As I was swimming, some young kids (and by young I mean probably under the age of 10) jumped into the pool and one of them, not paying any attention, landed right on top of me! I didn't know what had hit me as I took in mouthfuls of pool water and began flailing around, trying to stop coughing and staying above water. And then I felt strong arms around me, lifting me up, out of the water. As I gasped for air and coughed up water, I saw that my rescuer was a really, really cute guy who turned out to be one of the pool's lifeguards.

Northwoods hired YMCA lifeguards each summer to oversee the pool, and they were really needed, as my experience showed. Once on dry land, my mom came running up to make sure I was okay. I assured her that I was, and then Ethan—because that was his name—introduced himself and I had my first New England crush! His full name was Ethan Adams and he was going to be a senior at Haverhill High in the fall. He was tall, with dark curly hair, and had the bluest eyes I'd ever seen. And I won't go into his bod—it was just amazing, but I guess he'd have to be in good shape to be a lifeguard. We talked as much as we could that day, since he did have to keep a close eye on the swimmers in the pool.

When I had to leave at 4 p.m., he asked, "Abby, will you be here tomorrow?"

"I have no plans right now," I replied, "so yes, if the weather is nice, I'll come down."

"Can you give me your phone number in case it rains?"

And I did. I left with my mom and I felt happier than I had felt in at least six months—since I had found out about the move and my world had collapsed.

As luck would have it, it did rain the next day and the next. I guess that's what weather is like in Massachusetts. You never know what to expect. But Ethan did text me and we texted for almost a half-hour. Then we went on FaceTime. I told him about my life in Vegas, how different it was from Massachusetts, and how much I missed my old friends. He told me about his plans for his senior year: where he was planning to apply to college, how he played on the varsity football and baseball teams, and how much he loved living in a place where there were four seasons. By the time we got off the phone, I felt as though I had known him for years!

And that began our relationship. To be honest, I couldn't believe he didn't have a girlfriend. He was way too good-looking not to be in a relationship already, but he told me he had ended his last one with a girl from another high school about six months before. He explained that she was just not serious enough about her grades and couldn't understand why he always needed to study. I assured him that taking tough classes and getting good grades was a major focus of my life, so he didn't have anything to worry about when it came to that. We started seeing each other almost every day, either at the pool on nice days, or driving around the area when it wasn't one of his lifeguarding days. I got to see the beaches near Haverhill (I had never lived near ocean beaches before) and I have to admit, I was falling for this guy and even starting to enjoy my new home!

On days when I wasn't with Ethan, my mom and I would spend time together, as she began the process of decorating our new house. It needed a whole different type of "look" than our condo in Vegas, so sometimes we'd go shopping for the stuff we needed for the house, and I got to see what the area around Haverhill was like. It wasn't like Vegas, that's for sure. One cloudy afternoon, as we were driving through Haverhill, my Mom pulled over to the side of the street and parked.

"I want to show you something," she said as she took my hand and walked me to a small grassy park in the center of the city.

As I looked up, I saw a large bronze statue of a woman holding a hatchet, and pointing at something with her other hand. The statue read "Hannah Duston." The small plaque at its base read, "Her slaying of her captors."

"Abby, you know that my maiden name was Duston?" my mom asked.

"Of course I know that. It's my middle name too."

"Well, Hannah was my relative from way, way back in the 1600s, and this is the first statue ever erected to a woman in this country," she explained. She then went on to tell me the story of my ancestor who was captured by the Indians back in the 1600s, along with her infant and two other adults. The Indians took their prisoners to New Hampshire, just over the border from Haverhill, and killed her baby. Hannah waited until the Indians were sleeping, took a hatchet and killed ten of her captors, taking their scalps, escaping with the other prisoners and returning to Haverhill."

She continued, "The statue we're looking at is called 'A Mother's Revenge.' The actual hatchet she used is on display at the Haverhill Historical Society's museum."

I must admit I was blown away by this story. "Why didn't you ever tell me this before?"

"I guess I didn't think you'd appreciate your family's history, but now that we're back where we come from, I thought you should at least see who your ancestors were. We come from a long line of strong women, Abby. Don't ever forget that."

In the months to come, I would remember her words many times.

CHAPTER 3

ANOTHER GOOD THING HAPPENS

By now I was getting used to living in Haverhill, and also in Massachusetts. Between my mom and Ethan, I got to take day trips to see lots of places around the state, and the beauty of a New England summer was making me less unhappy about our move. I was on FaceTime with Julie every night, and when I sent her a selfie I took with Ethan, I thought she was just going to die!

"Oh my God, Abby, he is so hot!"

"I know, Jules, and I can't believe he likes me!"

"Why not? I told you you'd be popular when you got there," she said.

"I know, but I really didn't believe you."

But it was only mid-July, and there was a long way to go until school started. I still hadn't made any new girlfriends and hadn't seen any girls my age at the pool. Maybe they were all at camp or something. One afternoon, around 4 p.m., when I got home from the pool, my mom called me into the kitchen.

"Guess what, Abby?"

"Come on, Mom, don't make me guess."

"Look in the spare room."

And off I went, where I found the most completely adorable puppy I had ever, ever seen anywhere! I knelt down, picked him up gently and held his little body in my arms as he licked my face and snuggled into me, wagging his tail the whole time.

"Mom! Where did you get him? When did you get him? Is it a he or a she? I can't believe you finally got me a dog!"

Truthfully, I had asked for a dog since I had been old enough to even know what a dog was. I had always loved animals and had desperately wanted a dog, but my parents had told me that the desert was no place to raise a dog because you couldn't walk one in the hot weather.

For me, it was love at first sight! I named my puppy Charlie because it fit him so well and, after all, he was a Cavalier King Charles Spaniel. He was a gorgeous reddish color called "ruby" by the breeder, and he had just one touch of white on him, a stripe right down the center of his little face. I knew I would spend the rest of my summer training him and enrolling him in puppy classes at the local pet store. I couldn't wait to introduce him to Ethan.

The days passed by more quickly as I divided my time between going to the pool, spending time with Ethan and training Charlie. By the beginning of August, Charlie knew how to heel when we walked on a leash. He would sit on command and come when I called him. I think my mom was amazed at how quickly he was housebroken, but Charlie seemed to know that he was supposed to do his business on the grass and not in the house, and I made sure to take him outside immediately after he ate his meals. At four months old, he was getting bigger and smarter every day. Julie was so jealous when I sent her a photo of Charlie.

"Abby, I think he's even cuter than Ethan!" she gushed.

Northwoods was the perfect place for a dog. Although the homeowners' association rules didn't allow us to fence our yard, there was so much wooded area that I could walk Charlie around the neighborhood and he would find lots of places to explore. It was such a beautiful community. I especially liked that no two homes looked exactly the same. That made it so different from Las Vegas, where almost every home was tan stucco with a red tile roof. There were Colonials, like ours, but there were also cute homes that were single-story and mom told me they were called Cape Cod homes, or just "capes." The homes were painted a variety of colors, so it made everything look really pretty, and people planted flower gardens around their homes that added to the colorful display. Sidewalks ran throughout the entire development, so it was safe to walk from early morning until fairly late in the evening.

Charlie and I took lots of walks together. Owning a dog for the first time in my life was one of the most wonderful experiences I had ever had. It was all I had dreamed it would be, and Charlie was like a best friend with fur. He was my constant companion, and of course, he slept in my bed. Ethan and I would even take him on our drives, and when we walked him, everyone would just melt when they saw him and tell me how adorable he was. I think Charlie knew when people were admiring him because his little tail never stopped wagging!

CHAPTER 4

THE PROPHECY

One summer day when Ethan wasn't lifeguarding, we took a trip to Salisbury Beach. It was sort of how I pictured Coney Island must have looked, with all kinds of tacky souvenir stores selling tee shirts and cheap jewelry; fast food shacks selling junk food like cotton candy and soft ice cream cones; and games of chance where you could win large and ugly stuffed animals. We couldn't resist buying some greasy fried dough, dripping with butter, and eating it as we slowly walked down the street. As we wandered along, we came to a storefront advertising "Mme. Merganza," who would tell your fortune by either reading tarot cards or reading your palm. Ethan dared me to have my fortune told.

"No way," I replied.

"Abby, are you scared?"

"No, I just don't believe in that stuff!"

"Oh, come on, do it for fun. I will."

And so we both went into the little shop and had our fortunes told. Mme. Merganza seemed to be what everyone's idea of a fortuneteller should look like. She wore a flowing black skirt and a flowery blouse with big puffy sleeves. And she had long black hair with a bandanna around her head and big gold earrings. Her face didn't look old, but it didn't look young either. She looked as though she had been dressed for a part in a movie.

Ethan's fortune was pretty predictable. I think Mme. Merganza must have looked at him, seen how athletic he looked and just knew he'd go to college and play a sport. And that was just what she predicted for him. My fortune, however, was much weirder.

"I see you have come from a long distance," she said in a low voice, looking at my palm, "and you have a long road ahead of you."

"What do you mean? I just moved here."

"You will come to a great divide, and you will have to choose your path. That is all I can tell you now. You will need to be careful, Little One, very careful."

I had never believed in fortunetellers, but as Ethan paid for our visit, I felt shivers going up and down my spine, and I wanted to run as far away from Mme. Merganza's shop as I could get.

"What do you think she meant?" I asked Ethan, as we drove away from Salisbury.

"Hey, I thought you didn't believe in that stuff."

"Well, how did she know I came from far away?"

"Who knows? They make lots of guesses, based on all kinds of things. Maybe she heard you talking and could tell from your accent that you didn't come from here."

"What do you mean, **my** accent? You're the one with the accent!" We both laughed and I tried to put the fortuneteller's prophecy out of my mind. Although it faded as the days went by, it would come back to haunt me in the months ahead in ways I could never have imagined.

CHAPTER 5

WHAT TO DO?

My mom had hired a decorator to help her "do" our new home in an authentic New England Colonial style. This was something completely new to me. The patchwork quilts, four-poster beds and pillowy sofas with pretty flowered prints were such a drastic change from the sleek, modern style I had gotten used to in Las Vegas, and so were the colors. There were no more desert colors of beiges, creams, and grays. Now we had yellows, greens and blues going on. I had to admit, I really liked it. The house looked so cozy. And my new bedroom—painted a soft green, with its four-poster bed and beautiful handmade quilt and canopy—was like my personal little tented home. I sent a photo to all my friends back in Vegas, and they were completely amazed at how awesome it looked. Julie especially raved about it because she was so into home decorating.

"It's like a Colonial style! I love it!" she texted.

My friend Mia texted: "I'm super jealous! LOL! I've always wanted a bedroom like that!!"

So I guess I was feeling pretty good about things, even though I really missed my friends.

Things got a bit more complicated with Ethan though, but then I guess relationships always do. We were getting really close that summer. Really close. Sometimes after we'd been out late at a movie, he'd park and we'd make out and it got harder and harder to stop ourselves from going too far. Each time it was me who stopped us. I guess it's usually the girl who has to make that choice. But I had thought a lot about what I would do if this happened.

In fact, about two years before this, Julie and I had sort of made a pact. It wasn't like a virginity pact or an abstinence pact. Neither of us thought we'd want to stay virgins until our wedding night. But one weekend when her parents were away and I was staying overnight at her house, we found one of her mom's *Cosmopolitan* magazines and started reading the sex guide article "25 Hot Sex Tricks," about how to please men in bed. After we read it, we both were quiet for a few minutes and then we had a heart-to-heart talk that I will always remember. What we basically decided was that neither of us would have sex with a guy until we thought we were really in love with him. We'd never allow ourselves to be pressured into doing something we didn't feel ready to do, and I believe that pact helped me figure out what to do in my relationship with Ethan.

I told Ethan I really needed to talk to him when he had time and we could be alone.

"Uh, oh, this sounds serious," he joked, but he agreed to pick me up after football practice one hot afternoon in late July, and we drove up to the beach.

"Ethan, you know that I really do like you a lot," I began.

"Are you breaking up with me?" he immediately asked.

"Of course not! But I need you to understand how I feel, so we don't go through this every time we make out. I'm only 15, and I won't be 16 until January. I just don't feel ready for sex. Not yet. I know you want to and I understand that."

"Abby, I respect you and I would never hurt you."

"I get that, Ethan, but you have to know that I won't change my mind for quite a while, at least. I don't have a timetable, but I just know that I'm not ready. If you have to date other girls, I'll just have to understand because I can't give you what you want."

I sort of knew I was taking a chance, but I really felt as though I had to tell Ethan how I felt when it came to sex. I risked having him walk away from our relationship, but I had decided that there was no other way around this.

Luckily, he turned out to be really understanding and I breathed a sigh of relief when he replied, "I don't want to be with anyone else, Abby. You're the best thing that's happened to me in a long time, and if I have to wait, then I will."

And that's how it was. I think Ethan knew that if we were going to stay a couple, he'd just have to live with my decision. I knew it wasn't going to be easy for either one of us.

CHAPTER 6

STONE WALLS

E ach day that summer I got up, had my cup of coffee and a bagel, and took Charlie out for his first walk of the day. I had to get him out early because the days really got hot after about 10 a.m., so I tried to be up by 8 and out the door by 9. Charlie was always waiting by the door with his tail madly wagging, doing a little dance of happiness—that is, if you believe dogs can dance!

It was at about this time that I started noticing the low stone wall that ran almost parallel to the sidewalk, partially hidden in the woods. It was made of large stones—boulders really—lying on top of each other, with no cement holding them together (or whatever it is that holds stone walls together.) It looked really old, and most of the stones had green stuff growing on them, sort of like moss but I knew it wasn't moss. I knew what moss looked like. The wall interested me and I can't explain why I was drawn to it. It seemed to go on into the woods forever. I couldn't even see where it ended. There were places where it was only one or two large boulders high and other places where the wall was several feet in height. I asked my mom about it and her answer was sort of vague.

"Oh, those walls are all over New England. They've been around since Colonial times. You'll see them everywhere you go."

Colonial times. Now I was even more interested. Me, Abby Whittier, who was never the least bit interested in history, was suddenly delving into the history of stone walls in New England because I just had to know. Each time I walked Charlie by the place where the wall came closest to the side-walk, I felt some kind of force pulling me to follow the wall into the woods. It was really eerie. So I actually sat down and did some research on the sub-ject, and I wasn't even back in school yet! I Googled "New England Stone

Walls" and couldn't believe how many articles there were on the subject. I read as many as I could that night, before my eyes started closing and I felt myself nodding off.

What I learned didn't really explain the mysterious attraction I felt, but it did tell me a lot about who built these walls and why. The walls dated back to the 1600s when colonists arrived in the New World. They were mostly farmers trying to make a living, and they found when they tilled the soil, there were huge boulders underneath. Apparently, when glaciers formed during the ice age, they trapped many rocks inside them. When the glaciers finally melted, they dumped millions of tons of rocks all over New England. The farmers moved the boulders to their fence lines and laid them on top of each other. None of the walls were very high, because it was hard to lift them above shoulder height. Eventually these farmers moved west to escape the rocky soil they called "The Work of the Devil." Today, the walls look abandoned which, of course, they are. In many cases, only a few of the base stones are left, but it's against the law in many states and towns to remove these stones, and there's a national movement to preserve the stone walls as they are today.

I became even more intrigued now that I had an idea about how old the stone wall was that I saw every day. On the farmland that had now turned back into forest, I imagined those farmers trying to clear their land and finding these big, huge boulders. It must have been really hard to keep lifting them and dragging them over to their property line to make that wall. In my mind's eye, I could almost picture one of them as he tried to lift one of those giant rocks that made up the stone wall. It had probably been quite a bit higher than it was now, since it was obvious that the wall had fallen down in lots of places. I felt I had to go back and look at it more closely. I just had to.

CHAPTER 7

A SECRET DISCOVERY

The next day, I decided to try and follow the wall into the woods. Charlie and I went on our walk, as we usually did. But when we arrived at the place where the woods seemed to open into a clearing and the wall was closest to the sidewalk, I picked Charlie up, held him in my arms, and walked into the woods to see where the wall would lead us. I thought that carrying Charlie would be the best idea, since I had no idea what might be lying on the ground beneath the carpet of leaves, or if he might get thorns in his little paws.

The woods where we began the walk were very open, with the trees far apart and the sun shining down on the carpet of dead leaves, broken branches and green shoots growing out of the ground. However, as I made my way into the woods, following the wall, the trees grew closer together, so that the sunlight filtered through small gaps in the leaves and made patterns on the forest floor. Making my way through the trees and underbrush got more difficult the farther I walked into the woods. With the sun barely able to peek through the leaves, it also got much darker.

I kept walking for what seemed to be a very long time, as the wall led us farther and farther into the woods. There were places where the wall was as high as my waist, and other places where it was only as high as my calves. I felt the oddest sensation, as if I was meant to do this. Coming from Las Vegas, I'd never walked in a forest before, so this was a whole new experience for me. There were squirrels and chipmunks who would spot us and flee, and I could hear them chattering as they ran away. I could hear all kinds of birds in the trees above me, too. There must have been many different species because their calls were all different. The only one I could recognize was the constant "caw, caw" of a crow.

It was obvious that no one had walked in these woods, alongside this wall, for many, many years because there was no sign of any path. I had to work my way through brambles and low-hanging branches, trying to see ahead of me. I also tried to look back every so often to make sure that I could still see our housing development in the distance. I'd absolutely never want to get us lost in the woods. After we'd been following the wall for a while—I can't really guess how long—we came to another clearing. I stopped and put Charlie on the ground because my arms were getting a bit tired of holding him. I surveyed where we were and realized that I couldn't see the houses from there, but that was okay. We'd just follow the wall back to where we came from. I looked to see where the stone wall led from this point. It appeared to keep going on into the woods, as far as my eyes could see, with no end in sight.

"I guess that's it for today, Charlie," I murmured to my little dog. "Let's turn around and head for home."

Charlie looked at me as if he fully understood what I meant. I swear if I thought dogs could smile, Charlie was smiling. I really don't think he felt comfortable in those woods.

As I bent down to pick him up, my attention was caught by a bit of yellowed-looking paper that seemed to be sticking out from between two of the rocks. Now that is really, really strange, I thought. And once again that feeling overcame me. I absolutely had to get that paper out from between those rocks. Could I possibly lift the top rock to pull out the paper? I looked around and found a pretty sturdy-looking stick, figuring that I would use it as a wedge to move the rock just enough to pull out the paper. But the stick broke with my efforts. I decided that I'd have to return to this place and bring some sort of tool that would let me grab the piece of paper. I marked the place where I found the paper by placing two large fallen branches, crossed over each other, leaning against the stone wall. I had to be sure of finding it again.

I picked up Charlie, carefully followed the wall and finally arrived back where we'd started. Isn't it funny how it always seems shorter to go back to where you started than to head out when you don't know exactly where you're going? We continued the rest of our walk and got back to the house before 10 a.m.

The rest of that afternoon, instead of going up to the pool, I searched all over the house for something I could use to pry apart those rocks. I felt as though I was on a mission, and I can't explain it any other way. I looked through my dad's tools in the garage. All he had were wrenches, hammers, pliers and a saw. Then I looked at my mom's gardening tools and there it was, finally, the perfect thing to move the rock. I took the heavy metal trowel and managed to sneak it into the house without my mom seeing me, so I could avoid questions about what I was up to. My plan was to return to the clearing and use the trowel to get at the piece of paper. I had no idea what, if anything, was written on it. I just knew, somehow, that I was meant to find it. How did I know that? To this day, I can't explain how I knew that piece of paper was meant for me.

CHAPTER 8

THE NOTE

After we finished dinner, I couldn't wait any longer. You have to understand I had never really lied to my parents. I'd never needed to because I'd never gotten involved in anything like drinking or drugs. My parents trusted me, so for me to have to come up with a lie to cover up my actual destination was not an easy thing to do, but having Charlie was definitely helpful.

"I feel like taking Charlie out for an evening stroll," I said, as I got up from the dinner table. "He enjoys his walks so much and this time of day is so much cooler than the afternoons. I'll be back soon." I put Charlie on his leash and left the house, feeling as guilty as if I'd committed a crime.

When we got to the stone wall, I picked Charlie up again and carried him through the woods until we came to the clearing where I'd seen the piece of paper. I had put the trowel in my back pocket, and my tee shirt was covering it up. Now I put Charlie on the ground with a stern warning to "stay." I took out the trowel and found the scrap of paper right where I had left the crossed branches. I wedged the trowel between the two rocks and pushed down on the handle. A small space opened up, just enough for me to carefully slide the paper out from between them, and then the top rock came down hard against the one underneath it. The whole process took less than 10 seconds.

I stared at the piece of paper before I turned it over. It wasn't like any paper I'd ever seen. It looked like the pieces of parchment I'd seen in museums, yellowed and fraying at the corners, almost like a scrap of cloth. I took a deep breath and shivered. For some reason, I felt frightened. Then I turned the piece of paper over and read:

Abigail, Meete Me Heer at Nine to night. N.

I felt as though I couldn't breathe, as though the world had stopped spinning on its axis. The forest sounds faded away, and I sensed a force stronger than anything I'd ever experienced enveloping me. Then my mind suddenly clicked back to my surroundings. I grabbed Charlie and ran back, through the brambles and branches, following the wall, until we were on the sidewalk again. As I set him down, I put the note in my pocket. I realized that I'd left the trowel back in the woods, but nothing would have made me go back and retrieve it now. I took the long way around the circle to get back to our house. It gave me enough time to compose myself and act normally when we arrived home.

"Abby, did you and Charlie have a nice walk?"

"Mom, this is a great time to walk him. There's less traffic, it's much cooler, and he seems to get less distracted than when we go out in the morning. I may start doing this more often."

So I was into it now—full deception. I went up to my room, took out the note, studied it and tried to decide whether it was really meant for me and most important, was I going back to see if there was really someone named "N" and whether he had meant that note for me. I had a lot of thinking to do.

CHAPTER 9

THE IN-BETWEEN DAYS

I look back on the days between when I found the note and when I made a decision about what to do as a time when I experienced more inner conflict in my life than I'd ever had before. I'd placed the note in my jewelry box, underneath the velvet lining, and took it out several times a day, just to gaze at it and hold it again, as if it would give me the answers to my questions. Was the note really meant for me? Should I go back at 9 p.m.? What would happen to me if I did? Did I have the courage to find out?

Days passed. I was busy. I tried to act normally with my parents and with Ethan. I finally got to meet Ethan's sister Elizabeth, who'd been at soccer camp all summer. I guess I hadn't realized that we were the same age and would be in some of the same classes starting in the fall. Liz and I hit it off immediately, and the three of us went out to a movie and a quick dinner one night during that period of my inner turmoil.

After we dropped Liz off at Ethan's house and Ethan was taking me home, he asked, "Is everything OK? You seem sort of different, not like the carefree Abby you usually are."

"Of course, I'm fine! Maybe it's just thinking about starting school that has me a little worried. You know, making new friends, going to a new high school and all that."

"Don't waste your time worrying about it. You'll be fine. Everyone will love you, just like I do. And Liz. You know Liz now, and she thinks you're great! Believe me, you won't have any problems when school starts."

If he'd only known what was going on in my mind. But this was one crucial event I was going to have to handle on my own. My parents noticed the change in me too. Maybe I'm not very good at hiding my emotions; maybe it was because I'd never been forced to do anything like that before.

"Abby, are you all right? You seem so subdued."

"Mom, it's fine. Nothing's wrong. Really."

"Are you sure? Is it something to do with Ethan? You can tell me, you know. I'm always here to listen, if you need me."

"I know that. Honestly, though, everything is fine."

After three days of constantly thinking about the note and what it meant, I finally came to a decision. I'd have to somehow overcome my fear and go back to see if anyone would come to that stone wall at 9 p.m. Since I had no way of knowing when the note had been written, how long ago it had been placed between the rocks, or what actual date that 9 p.m. time was even meant for, I decided that I just had to take a chance and go there to see what would happen. Once again, I had to use my newfound deception techniques to get away from the house. I told Ethan I was feeling tired and didn't feel like going out. I told my parents that Ethan and Liz were picking me up at the clubhouse and that we were going to a party at a house in Hampton Beach, New Hampshire, a fun place to go in the summer. I just hoped they'd have no reason to compare notes.

At 8:45, wearing jeans and a tank top, I started out towards the stone wall. It was a really hot night. I had a small flashlight in my back pocket, one of those LED ones, to help me navigate the woods in the darkness. I'd also sprayed myself with bug spray because I couldn't afford to go home covered in scratches from the brambles and branches I'd be going through, or covered in mosquito bites. It might raise way too many questions. Those woods were so gloomy and dark at night, even under a full moon. I'd never felt scared when I walked in there with Charlie in the daylight, but now, all alone, with the darkness closing in on me the further into the woods I traveled, I felt fearful. It was not just fear of what might be lurking in the woods, but a deeper fear of what might happen when I got to that clearing. I didn't have much further to go, and then I finally arrived. I knew it was the place because there, on the ground, was the trowel I'd mistakenly left behind the day I'd gotten the note out from between the rocks.

I stood there in the clearing, next to the rock wall. At that point the wall was very low, maybe only a foot high. The moon was shining overhead and even though I couldn't see the houses in our development, I could see the illumination cast by the many streetlights in the neighborhood. It calmed my fear just a tiny bit. Then, as I looked into the woods beyond the wall, I saw him. A man was standing far away in the distance. He appeared to be almost shimmering in the glow of the moonlight as he beckoned to me. I thought he looked to be about my age, but he was dressed in old-fashioned clothes and his hair was dark and curly. I wanted to turn around and run away, but a strange feeling overcame me, as though a force was surrounding me and reassuring me that I would be safe. I turned back, and now I heard him calling, softly, almost as if his voice were coming to me from a faraway place.

"Abigail, cross over the wall. Please, Abigail, come over here to me." And then he repeated his words, "Abigail, please cross over the wall."

The force I had felt enveloping me had left me unable to resist. I took a deep breath and with one step, I crossed over the stone wall.

CHAPTER 10

A DIFFERENT ME

As I took a step over to the other side of the wall, I heard a roaring sound in my ears, as though I was traveling at high speed, tumbling through a long tunnel. A blinding flash of light forced me to close my eyes. Fear overwhelmed me as I set both feet down and stood there trembling, rooted to the spot, not knowing what was happening to me. Eventually the noise died down and I slowly opened my eyes, terrified of what I might see.

There he was, holding his hands out to me, as if to take my hands in his. He was smiling a brilliant smile and I felt my fears dissolve when I heard his voice. It was a voice I felt I'd heard many times before.

"Abigail, how long I have waited here, each night, with the hope that you would find my note and return to our meeting place."

I looked at him then and realized he was no longer an insubstantial, shimmering figure, but a flesh and blood person, with curly dark hair, tied back, and brilliant blue eyes, dressed in the knee-length pants, stockings and shirt of an American Colonist like the pictures I'd seen in my U.S. history book. Where was I? I turned around to see whether the streetlights of Northwoods were still visible. To my shock, the woods were no longer there, nor was there any sign of a housing development. Instead, I saw what appeared to be farmland, stretching from the stone wall as far as my eyes could see. I turned back to the stranger.

"My name is Abigail, but I'm not the person you've been waiting for," I stammered. "I have no idea who you are or why you've been waiting for me."

As I said this, I reached for my hair, a gesture I often make when I'm nervous. To my complete amazement, I found that my head was covered instead in some sort of cap with streamers hanging from it. When I looked down,

I realized that the jeans and tank top I had worn into the woods had been transformed into a long skirt made of some kind of woolen or linen material, a white blouse with puffy sleeves, and a vest made of the same material as the skirt. What had happened to me?

"Abigail, you have been gone for so terribly long. You vanished and I thought you were never coming back to me. I am Nathaniel White, and we were the dearest of friends before you disappeared. Was it that you were captured by the Indians? Have you perhaps been ill? Many here were taken away by the throat distemper. I kept coming to our meeting place, and each night I prayed to the Almighty that you might be restored to me."

My astonishment knew no bounds! "Nathaniel, I am Abigail Whittier but I have no memory of our time together. I don't know what year it is here, but I come from a different time. I don't dress in clothes like these and there are no Indians where I live. We don't even call them Indians in our time. They're known as Native Americans. I don't know what has happened to me, but it must have something to do with that stone wall. That's where I found your note."

"Abigail Whittier—of course I **know** that is your name. You are here in 1763, and the Treaty of Paris has just been signed to put an end to the war between England and France. You must have been very, very ill with convulsion fitts to believe you come from a future time. Walk with me so that we can overcome your fear and I can deliver you from this affliction."

At this point, I took Nathaniel's hand and started walking with him. I didn't understand what had happened, but somehow I knew that I needed to find out what this other Abigail Whittier's life had been like. I couldn't stay in this long-ago world, but I also knew that Nathaniel had been waiting for me. He knew me, and I had somehow been transported back in time to meet him. My rational mind told me this wasn't possible, yet here I was, and I was definitely not in the world I knew. As we walked along together, hand in hand, I began to feel more comfortable.

"Nathaniel, how old are you and are you in school?"

"Abigail, I am 16 years of age and have been working on my father's farm since I was 14. Have you no memory of any of this?"

"No, I really don't remember. I feel as though I know you, or I did know you, but I don't recall any details of this life. Where are my parents?"

At this point, Nathaniel stopped walking and turned to me. "Abigail, it pains me to deliver you news that your parents were killed in an Indian raid. You must have escaped, but your whereabouts have been unknown. All who survived asked about you up and down the colony, but no one could say where you might be."

I was speechless, unable to come up with even one more question. I knew I had to return to my home, and I hoped that crossing back over the stone wall would reverse the whole process. I had not thought about what I would do if I couldn't go back to my "real life."

"Nathaniel, I must go now."

"Abigail, will you come back? How I have missed you. Now that I have found you again, I beg, do not leave me waiting here as I have done for the last long year."

"I will try to return, Nathaniel. I promise I will try. But I have a much different life now and I have to think about that. I will try to come back and then I can explain more to you about the world I live in."

We walked back to the stone wall, hand in hand. I looked up at Nathaniel, at his loving gaze, and I knew that I really did want to return and see him again. I stopped for a brief moment, without thinking, to pick up a button that seemed to have fallen from Nathaniel's shirt, but now I turned away from him and slowly stepped back over the wall. Once again, I heard the roaring sound and closed my eyes against the blinding light. As I opened my eyes, I felt my head. My hair was just as it had been, loose and long, not covered by a cap. I looked down and saw my jeans and tank top, and here I was in the woods. I breathed a sigh of relief.

I turned around and looked back across the stone wall and saw Nathaniel, slowly fading from my sight. As he did, he waved. I could almost feel his sadness.

CHAPTER 11

'X' MARKS THE SPOT

I stood motionless next to the wall. Time passed. I knew I had to go home. I looked at my wrist, and my watch was there again. I realized that while I thought my time with Nathaniel had been at least an hour or two, my trip back in time had only lasted about 15 minutes in our world. I couldn't imagine how this could be. Maybe traveling into the past made time pass more quickly, even when it seemed to take place exactly as it did here. My confusion deepened. What I knew for sure was that I couldn't speak about any of this, not to anyone. Who would believe me? Definitely not my parents. They would have me on a psychiatrist's couch in a flash!

I made sure to mark the place where I had crossed over the wall using the crossed branches I had left the last time. I was afraid I wouldn't find the exact place again. Would the entire length of the wall let me travel back in time, or was it just this one spot? Using my mother's trowel, I dug a hole and stuck the branches in so they stood upright in the air. There'd be no mistaking them. I buried the branches deep enough so they wouldn't fall over in the wind, and then I turned and started walking back along the wall, back towards home. Since it wasn't 10 p.m. yet, I knew I'd need a cover story about coming home so early…more lies. I told myself I had no choice.

"Abby! We didn't expect you home for several hours!"

It figured this would be one of the few Saturday nights my parents had decided to stay home.

"Ethan and I left the party early when we saw people bringing in a keg of beer," I explained. "He has to be really careful about any issues of substance abuse or he could be suspended from the football team. We just decided to call it a night. I'm really tired, so I'm just going upstairs to watch some TV in bed."

"Sure, Sweetheart, if you're tired, that's a good thing. Do you want a snack or anything to take upstairs with you?"

"No, I'm good. Thanks, though, Mom." And I walked upstairs as though I hadn't a care in the world.

Once I was in my room, I lay on my bed and allowed myself to relive what I'd experienced that night. Part of me rejected the whole thing. I told myself it was a dream, that I'd been overtired and had imagined the entire incident, maybe because I'd been reading too much about the early Colonial history of Haverhill and about the stone walls. I didn't believe in time travel. I never read science fiction. Things like that just don't happen. I got up from my bed and went over to my jewelry box. Reaching in carefully, under the velvet lining, I touched the piece of parchment I'd found between the rocks. There it was. It was real. At least I hadn't imagined that someone with the initial "N" had asked someone named "Abigail" to meet him at the stone wall at 9 p.m. I didn't make that up.

I decided to get ready for bed and watch a little TV to take my mind off the night's events. As I undressed, something fell out of my jeans pocket. I bent down to grab it. It was the button, the one I had picked up and put in the folds of the skirt I was wearing, just before I had crossed back over the wall. I looked at it closely. It was like no other button I had ever seen. As I looked at the button even more closely, I thought it seemed to have been made by hand, with many, many stitches covering the outside of the button to make it rigid. I realized that I now had a piece of evidence I could use to figure out whether my time-travel experience had actually taken place.

CHAPTER 12

EVIDENCE EXAMINED

The next morning I got up early and decided to pursue this evidence before any more time had passed.

"Mom, didn't you say that there were actual artifacts of Hannah Duston at the Haverhill Historical Museum?"

"You know, that's what I've been told, but I've never been there. Somehow we've never found the time to check that out in all the trips we've made to Massachusetts, and now that we're actually living in Haverhill, I suppose I should find out if it's true."

"It's raining today," I replied. "Can we take a ride over to the Historical Society and find out if we can see the Hannah Duston exhibit?"

"Sure, let me check online to see their hours, and if they're open today, we can go over there. I have a hair appointment, but if you want to stay longer, I can pick you up later. I'm just getting a quick trim. Your father and I have a dinner party tonight, so I thought I'd get my hair looking better than it has been."

"That's great! I'll run upstairs and get dressed while you check on the museum hours!"

Later that morning, mom and I went to the Haverhill Historical Society, also known as The Buttonwoods, and it was a really amazing place! Apparently, according to the director, members of the Duston family come from all over the country to see the Hannah Duston exhibit. Of course, most of them are interested in seeing the hatchet that she used to scalp the Indians, but I really thought that was sort of bloodthirsty. My favorite item in the exhibit was her

"Profession of Faith." It was a document welcoming her into the church, but since she couldn't sign her own name, it was signed for her and she just placed an "X" where her signature should have been.

Since my mother had to leave for the hair salon, I decided to stay awhile, knowing I had other business to take care of. There were so many things to see besides the Hannah Duston exhibit that I knew I wouldn't run out of things to interest me. But first I approached the museum's director once I was sure my mother had driven out of the parking lot. I reached into my pocket and took out the button that had fallen from Nathaniel's shirt. Holding it in my hand—this one small reminder of last night's adventure—I asked, "Have you ever seen a button like this before?"

The director's eyes widened as she took the button from my hand. "Of course, we have many of these types of buttons in our collection. They're linen thread buttons and were the easiest and cheapest buttons to make in Colonial times when most families made their own clothes. But finding one like this, in pristine condition, actually new-looking, that's truly an amazing thing! Where did you come across it?"

I explained that it had been wedged between two rocks in a stone wall in our nearby woods, and had caught my eye. Honestly, I had been totally unprepared for the question, and I knew my answer sounded suspicious. I hadn't really gotten to the point where I believed what had happened last night, so her answer shook me to my core.

"Do you want us to keep it here, or were you planning to hold on to it?" The director seemed unable to tear her gaze away from the button.

"No, I'd like to keep it for awhile," I replied, "but ultimately, I'll probably donate it to the museum. Don't worry, I'll keep it in a special box with my grandmother's ring."

That seemed to satisfy her and she went back to her computer work, while I looked at other exhibits, waiting for my mother to pick me up. My adventure in time travel was no longer just a figment of my imagination. Each time I looked at that button, I was eager to step over the wall and see Nathaniel again.

CHAPTER 13

REAL LIFE INTERFERES

The next morning dawned cloudless, sunny and very warm. I decided to take Charlie out for his walk as early as possible because the day promised to be a scorcher. As soon as I had my breakfast, I put him on his leash as he danced around madly, eager to get outdoors. We walked our usual route and I must admit, I felt a sense of foreboding as I approached the clearing where the stone wall was. I decided I had to overcome my fear, so grasping Charlie firmly under my arm, I walked into the clearing and stood in front of the wall. It was not too high here—maybe two feet at the most. Closing my eyes and taking a deep breath, I stepped over it. Nothing happened. There was no flash of light, no roaring sound in my ears. In fact, I couldn't hear a thing except some birds chirping in the woods. I turned around and stepped back over the wall and continued our walk around the neighborhood, arriving home in time to catch my mom leaving for the pool.

"Can you wait a few minutes so I have time to change into my bathing suit?"

"Sure, Hon, do you want me to bring that small cooler with some bottles of water for us?"

"That'd be great! I'll be right down!"

I ran upstairs, changed into my suit, grabbed a big beach towel and my sunscreen and visor, and ran back downstairs. I was looking forward to spending a sunny day, probably one of the last before school started, hanging out at the pool with Ethan, swimming and tanning. Later on in the week I had an appointment to register for classes, so I wanted to talk to him and to Liz, if she was there, about which teachers were the best for each subject.

It really was a perfect summer day. I spent lots of time with Ethan who had cut down on his lifeguarding so he could practice with the football team. Liz and I talked non-stop about the high school, the classes I planned to sign up for, and the teachers to absolutely avoid. By 3:30, I was so tired I just had to go home and take a nap. I guess the emotional upheaval I had been going through had worn me down.

As I lay in my bed, I thought about my morning walk with Charlie and how crossing over the wall had led me nowhere. I was puzzled by this, but worked out that the spot where I had been able to cross over into a long lost time must only exist at that one specific place along the wall. I was definitely going back there, but it couldn't be tonight. I was going out to dinner with Ethan, and he had planned to take me into Boston—something I had only done one or two other times since moving to Massachusetts.

The dinner turned out to be a double date because Liz brought her boyfriend Josh along. We drove into the new Seaport District and ate the most delicious seafood I have ever tasted at a place right on the water. I think a former Red Sox player owned it. One thing I had learned by now was that New Englanders were really crazy about their sports teams, and Red Sox fans were completely crazy when it came to anything to do with their beloved Sox. Ethan promised that he'd try to get us tickets if the Sox made the playoffs. Since Las Vegas didn't have any major league teams, I had never been to a real pro baseball game. The three of them couldn't believe it when I confessed to this missing piece in my life.

I got home way too late to go to the stone wall that night, so I promised myself that I would definitely go the next night. I didn't know whether Nathaniel would be there, but if I didn't see him in the distance, I wouldn't try to make the crossing. I decided that the next time I went to the wall, I would bring a daily newspaper to see if it would cross over with me. Neither my clothes nor my watch had made the crossing, but Nathaniel's button did make the crossing back, so I decided it would be worth a try. Maybe if Nathaniel could see the news of today, he would believe that I was a different Abigail from the one he had been waiting for.

CHAPTER 14

MY SECOND CROSSING

My mom and I kept our appointment at the high school early the next morning so I could get registered for classes. I couldn't believe how small the high school was, compared with the one I had gone to in Las Vegas. But then again, Haverhill is a small city of around fifty thousand people, while Las Vegas has several million people, so I should have expected the high school to be much smaller. I loved my new guidance counselor, Mrs. Janvier. She had a folder all set up for me and had already gone over my records from Palm Desert High School.

"Welcome to Haverhill High, Abby! I can see you'll want to sign up for some of our Advanced Placement courses this year, right?"

"Definitely," I replied. "What do you suggest? I don't want to take too many because I'm hoping to play sports and maybe join some clubs to get to know people."

After Mrs. Janvier went over the courses available to juniors with my mom and me, I enrolled in two AP courses: British Lit and American History, and then took the rest of my subjects at the honors level. It wasn't going to be an easy year for me, but I was used to studying hard and I had goals. I hoped to be able to go back to Las Vegas for college at the University of Nevada, Las Vegas. I hadn't told my parents about that yet. I guessed they were probably hoping I'd want to stay in New England for college. By the time we had a tour of the high school and I got my schedule, it was early afternoon. Mom and I decided the pool was our best bet since the weather was what the weathermen in Massachusetts called the three H's: hazy, hot and humid. I lazed around the pool, swam some laps and talked to Ethan and Liz about my schedule. Things seemed to be coming together, at least on the outside. No one knew what was going on in my mind as I thought about the stone wall and my trip into New England's past.

After dinner that night, I managed to find the day's *Boston Globe*, lying in the recycle bin. I carefully ripped off the front page, folded it tight, and stuffed it in the back pocket of my jeans. I was determined to try and convince Nathaniel that I was not the Abigail he knew—that I was from a different time—and if I showed him the newspaper, with its modern date and stories, he would have no choice but to believe me.

As it started getting dark, I sprayed myself with bug spray and yelled, "I'll be back soon!" as I quickly ran out the back door. I jogged to the clearing and then began following the stone wall, making sure to keep my flashlight ready for when the forest became darker. I reached my destination fairly quickly this time, probably because I was starting to wear a path through the brush. I found my crossed sticks marking the spot on the wall and as I looked into the distance, I saw Nathaniel again, shrouded in mist. As I focused on him, I saw him waving at me, beckoning me to come to him. Wrapping my arms around myself, trying to prepare for what was to come, I stepped over the wall.

I wish I could fully describe what it feels like to travel back in time. All I can say is that it felt as though I were falling through a long, long tunnel very, very fast. The deafening "whooshing" noise in my ears, along with the blinding flash of light that forced me to close my eyes, all seemed to overcome me at once. And then, in an instant, they stopped and there I was. Just as with my first experience, I was no longer wearing my jeans and t-shirt, but was wearing the clothing and head covering of Colonial times. Nathaniel was there, waiting for me and so happy to see me again.

"Abigail, you have returned! I was so fearful that you would disappear into the mist." He took my two hands in his.

Now I reached into the pocket of the linen skirt to see if the newspaper had crossed over the wall with me. It was there!

"Nathaniel, you must understand that I am not the Abigail you know, but someone from another time, many hundreds of years in the future. I have brought something to prove it to you."

I brought out the newspaper and unfolded it, but as I did, I watched as the ink rapidly faded and disappeared until, as I went to show it to Nathaniel, the page was simply a blank sheet of newsprint. I was shocked! How could this happen? I just didn't understand it at all.

"Abigail, I fear I shall only be able to meet you one or two more times before I must leave. A militia is being formed in Lexington. The British Governor has subjected our colony to harsh laws, and it is the belief of many righteous men that someday soon, we colonists must rise up and oppose the unjust edicts of the King."

"I know all about that, Nathaniel. You must be speaking of The Stamp Act—the tax levied on printed paper by King George."

"Abigail, how is it possible for you to know that? Since the Treaty in 1763, the Crown hast tried our loyalty and not recognized our contribution to the victory over the French. King George tries to pay his huge debts on the backs of the colonists."

"Nathaniel, you may not believe me, but you must try. The colonists will fight a war of independence against the British and they will win. The colonies will form the beginning of a new country—my country, the United States of America. This is the truth. In the year I live in, there are fifty states. Fifty! People from the first colonies spread west and covered all of the continent from East to West, from the Atlantic Ocean to the Pacific. The country now has over 300 million people."

We walked and talked like this for what seemed like hours. I told Nathaniel about George Washington, about the Declaration of Independence and the Constitution and tried to explain about cars and televisions. I thought I should wait to explain about airplanes because I didn't want to overwhelm him. I could see the doubt in his eyes, but he still hung on my every word.

"Abigail, if it is true that you have come to me from another time, then surely there must be a reason why the Almighty has seen fit in his wisdom to send you here to me. I cannot imagine what your life must be like when I listen to the world you describe. If you will stay here in my world and become my betrothed, I can offer you a life as my dearest wife, after I return from my militia training. My father will provide me with enough land to farm and we will build a home to raise our children. I would pledge myself to you now, if you would have me."

"Nathaniel, I'm only fifteen and won't turn sixteen until January. Girls in my time do not marry until they are in their twenties or thirties, sometimes even older. I'm way too young to marry now."

"Abigail, in our time, people do not always live to the age of thirty. We must marry at an early age to have children to carry on our family name. If you did not cross back over the wall and stayed here with me, I would do everything within my power to ensure your happiness. I beg you to consider my proposal."

I looked at Nathaniel sadly, knowing in my heart that what he was asking just could not be. And yet, a part of me wished to stay here longer with this man. I felt dread, knowing that someday soon I might lose him forever. As I turned to go, I was seized by an irresistible impulse and I quickly turned back and kissed him. He, in turn, put his strong arms around me and looked longingly into my eyes.

"Nathaniel, I have to go now. I'll try to return soon. You must not think of marriage to me. It's not a question of love. We come from two different times and I don't think either one of us can change that."

With that I walked over to the wall, closed my eyes and stepped back over, feeling everything I had felt before, and even though I should have become used to it by now, I was still terrified. I opened my eyes to see the woods again, with the Northwoods streetlights in the distance. Looking back into the woods, across the wall, I saw Nathaniel, once again shrouded in mist, walking away from me.

CHAPTER 15

MY DILEMMA

As I mentioned before, I had never lied to my parents until now. I had always thought of myself as someone who tried to be an honest person. Deception and lying were never a part of my personality. But now I found myself lying not only to my parents, but deceiving Ethan and even Julie. My conscience was really bothering me. I tried to figure out what to do. I never really considered telling any of them about crossing over the wall and finding myself in Haverhill back in Revolutionary War times. All of them would have thought I was losing my mind and I wouldn't have blamed them. If it hadn't happened to me, and someone had told me that story, I would have thought they were crazy.

What bothered me the most were my feelings for Nathaniel. While I knew there was no possibility of ever having any kind of relationship with him beyond our few brief meetings when I crossed over the stone wall, I did care for him. I felt a connection to this man that I just could not explain to myself. That made me feel guilty because in a way, I was seeing someone else behind Ethan's back. It didn't seem right.

I had never had a serious boyfriend before. Ethan was the first guy I had gone out with exclusively, and I knew he thought of us as a couple. I thought of us that way too. We seemed right for each other and never had the everyday fights that other couples seemed to have. I loved being with him and always looked forward to seeing him. So why was I drawn to that stone wall and why did I feel the connection to Nathaniel? I hoped that as time passed, I would come to understand this better. I knew that whatever happened, I didn't want anything to come between Ethan and me. I finally decided that meeting

Nathaniel couldn't be considered cheating on Ethan because it wasn't happening in today's world. I had made it very clear to Nathaniel that despite any feelings I had for him, there could be no future for us. He had accepted that fact, although it had made him sad.

Those were the conclusions I had reached after lots of thinking late at night, as I was lying in my bed trying to fall asleep. I made my peace with my conscience and hoped that my relationship with Ethan would stand the test of time. My feelings for him were growing stronger every day.

CHAPTER 16

A NEW SCHOOL YEAR

Haverhill High School began right after Labor Day and I was caught up in the frenzy of books, laptops, teachers, assignments and meeting new people. For someone like me who had spent her entire life growing up in the same place, it was a completely mind-blowing experience! I tried to remember everyone's names, but it was impossible, and the homework and assignments began from day one. It was clear that the teachers' expectations in the honors and AP classes were high—much higher than what had been expected of me in my Las Vegas high school. But then, I had seen the statistics many times that showed that Massachusetts was at the top of all the states when it came to education. Students scored higher here, and I guess it was because teachers pushed harder.

Luckily it wasn't all hard work. I made some new friends quickly thanks to Liz. She was awesome in academics and sports, and she introduced me to all her friends. That just made things so much easier. I had kids to eat lunch with, kids I knew in my classes, and kids I could text if I didn't understand an assignment. During my free period, I was part of a small study group that met in the library where we had coffee, courtesy of the librarians, and helped each other prepare for tests. By the third week of classes, I felt as though I had gone to school here all my life.

I still went on FaceTime with Julie at least two or three times a week. I don't think anyone could ever break the bond between us. She was happy that I was adjusting to my new life and we made plans for her to come visit me over Christmas vacation. I wanted to go back to Las Vegas for a visit, but since Julie had never been to Massachusetts or to the East Coast, she desperately wanted to visit me. So I gave in and we arranged it with our parents. I couldn't even put into words how much I wanted to see my best friend again. I missed her so much; I especially missed the way we could just talk for hours about absolutely anything.

The homecoming football game and dance were going to take place on the second Saturday night in October and, of course, Ethan asked me to go with him. I had planned on going to all of the football games to cheer on the Haverhill Hillies, and I was excited to be going to my first homecoming dance at my new high school with my boyfriend who just happened to be captain of the football team!

I walked Charlie early in the morning, before Ethan picked me up for school, and then again in the late afternoon when I got home from soccer practice. Oh yes, I had managed to make the team, with a little bit of a push from Liz, who sang my praises to the coach. I was a back-up goalie, and that was fine with me. Between academics, soccer practice, taking care of Charlie, and hanging out with my new friends, my life was filled to the brim. But still, I thought about Nathaniel in spare moments throughout each day, and as I walked Charlie past the stone wall, I planned my next trip back in time to meet him.

CHAPTER 17

A REAPPEARANCE

Believe it or not, one of the many changes I had to get used to was fall. You see, when I was growing up in the desert, there really was nothing like fall in New England. While my parents had described how the weather would gradually get cooler and the leaves would turn color, I guess it's one of those things you really have to experience for yourself to understand. Incredibly, just as school started after Labor Day weekend, I noticed the difference in the temperature, both early in the morning and in the late afternoons when I took Charlie on his walks. There was definitely a "nip in the air," as people said here, and for me, it seemed exciting! As September continued along, the leaves began turning colors very gradually, and I thought it was amazing! Four seasons. Everyone else took it for granted, but Ethan and Liz thought it was hysterical how excited it made me.

One afternoon, I met Ethan after his football practice and my soccer practice were over, and he asked about my plans for the coming weekend.

"Really, I'm just planning on going to the football game, and that's about it, unless you have other ideas," I told him.

"Well, this Saturday is the Italian Festival downtown," he explained, "and it's really a great time! There are all kinds of booths and food, and I know you'll really like it. Want to go?"

"Sure! Sounds like a blast!"

And so, we made plans for Ethan to pick me up after the game ended.

Saturday came around, bright, crisp, and sunny—a perfect fall day. The football game was at home and the Hillies' stadium was filled to capacity because our team was really doing well this year. Liz and I and some other friends got there early, got great seats and cheered our Hillies on to victory—their second win of the season. I was really enjoying fall in my new little city!

Around 1 o'clock, Ethan picked me up and we drove downtown for the Italian Festival. He had to park pretty far away, since it had started earlier in the day, but there were all kinds of activities going on, and the delicious smells of Italian food made my mouth water. We stopped at several of the food booths without buying anything but a Coke, and then we sat down on a bench to try and decide what we wanted to eat. Caught up in our discussion of whether to get meatball subs or lasagna, I suddenly felt a shadow fall over us and looked up. And there she was, the fortuneteller we had gone to in Salisbury Beach, back in the summer, Mme. Merganza. She was dressed in the same unique clothing she had been wearing when we had met her at the beach, but she didn't stand out in the crowded Italian Festival because there were many people wearing colorful costumes, mingling throughout the downtown area.

It seemed like ages ago that we had had our fortunes told, and to be honest, her prophecy had puzzled me at first and maybe even scared me a little. However, I had been so busy since moving to Massachusetts that I really hadn't had time to dwell on it. Now, though, it all came flooding back and I felt a sense of dread.

"Hello, Madame Merganza," I stammered, "it's nice to see you here in Haverhill. You probably don't remember us, but you told our fortunes up in Salisbury Beach this past summer."

"Ah yes," she replied, "of course I remember you, Little One. I had hoped to see you again sometime in the future to see if my warning had helped you."

"What warning?" Ethan asked.

"It was nothing serious," I assured him. "Madame Merganza, I really am fine, and while I appreciate that you were concerned about me and remembered me, I honestly think your concern was unnecessary."

"I see what I see, Little One. Again I tell you that when the path divides, you must be sure to take the one that leads you back to your home that you know and love so well." With that, she whisked away around a corner and we were left feeling a sense of disbelief.

"Did that really happen?" Ethan asked. "What on earth was she talking about? Do you have any idea what path she means?"

Of course it had all become clear to me now, but I could never, ever let Ethan know the truth.

"Ethan, don't tell me you're the one who's the believer in fortune-telling now," I teased him. "Come on, let's get some lunch. I'm starving!"

We ended up buying some of the most delicious lasagna I think I've ever tasted and enjoyed every last bite. It was only after Ethan had dropped me off at three o'clock, with the promise of picking me up later to go to a house party, that I had time to think about Mme. Merganza's very perceptive warning and what it really meant. If I hadn't believed in fortune telling before, I was definitely becoming a believer. It seemed there were many things that would never have seemed possible to me before, that were becoming real to me now.

Life is definitely strange, I thought to myself, as I tried to decide what to wear to the party that night.

CHAPTER 18

CONFIDING IN A FRIEND

Ethan and I had a great time at the party Saturday night! I have to admit that I loved spending time with him and he had kept his word after our summer talk and hadn't pressured me to have sex, even though we did have some pretty heavy make out sessions. He was smart, funny and athletic, and we had a lot in common. By now, I had met his parents and they had made me feel welcome in their home. All in all, it was the best relationship I could have imagined having in high school.

When I was alone, however, thoughts of Nathaniel intruded. I would go to the lining in my jewelry box and take out his note and the button from his shirt and just stare at them, trying to understand how my time travel could actually happen. It didn't make sense to me, yet I had these very real items to prove to me that what I had experienced was not a figment of my imagination. I had an intense desire to talk about this with someone.

Looking for answers to something that seemed impossible, I went to my laptop and Googled "time travel." I couldn't believe how many different articles popped up. I decided to try the one on Wikipedia to see if there was anything that would help me understand what was going on. Unfortunately, the very long article was so technical that even though I tried to figure out what it meant, I really didn't have the knowledge of physics that was needed. The few sentences I could make sense of told me that very famous and brilliant people like Albert Einstein and Stephen Hawking had spent time considering and writing about the possibility of time travel. One sentence really jumped out at me, "The theory of general relativity does suggest a scientific basis for the possibility of backward time travel in certain unusual scenarios." The article also explained that compared to other concepts in physics, the concept of time was still not understood very well. What I knew from my own experience was that items from the past, like the note and Nathaniel's button, could make the crossing into the present, but things from the present, like the newspaper page, could not cross over into the past.

I finally decided that during one of my FaceTime sessions with Julie, I would bring up the subject of time travel to see what she would say. We had always shared every detail of our lives with each other, and yet I had kept this very important event a secret from her. While I wasn't sure exactly how to bring up the subject, I made up my mind that I would just do it. A few nights later, Julie and I were having a heart-to heart talk about her latest crush when I brought up the subject.

"Jules, do you believe people can travel back in time?" I asked.

"What do you mean, Abby? Like really going back to a different time in history?"

"Yeah, like taking a trip back into the past and meeting people who lived hundreds of years ago. Do you think that's possible?"

"Abby, what in the world is happening to you? Is living in New England making you crazy? Are you having weird dreams? I have never, ever heard you talk about anything like this!"

"No, Jules, I was just thinking about all the people who lived here in Colonial times, how we read about them in history books, and how awesome it would be if there were a way we could go back and actually meet them. I guess it's a silly thought."

"Silly? Abby, honestly, I am worried about you. I can't believe you even think of things like that! Come on, Girl, stop this right now!"

So I had my answer. Julie, my best friend in the whole world, would rather think I was losing my mind than consider the possibility that time travel could be real. I decided not to ever bring up the subject to anyone else (that is, until I decided to write this account of my experience.)

CHAPTER 19

CROSSING AGAIN

It had been a busy few weeks since school started and while I had been thinking quite often about the stone wall and seeing Nathaniel, I hadn't been able to find enough time to cross over the wall and meet him again. Complicating matters was the fact that the daylight hours were getting shorter, although it had always seemed to be daylight in Nathaniel's world, no matter what time it was when I made the crossing.

I still hadn't been able to figure out the time difference between Nathaniel's world and mine. My watch, along with my clothes, did not make the crossing with me, so I couldn't really tell how long I spent in his world, but I could estimate. I knew that I had spent well over an hour or two in Colonial times, yet when I crossed back over the wall and looked at my watch, only a short time had elapsed. And in-between my crossings, several years had passed in Nathaniel's life but only a few days had gone by in mine. Time travel was a mysterious concept—way beyond my understanding, that's for sure.

The woods somehow seemed more frightening in the fall, maybe because the bright shiny green leaves and wildflowers of summer were no longer there. Instead, many of the leaves had turned colors and some had already fallen to the forest floor during one of the frequent rainstorms we'd been having. That was another big difference I noticed between Las Vegas and Massachusetts: rain. Sometimes it seemed as though it rained almost every day. I explained to my new friends that you could count the number of rainy days per year in Las Vegas on one hand, so having it be wet and gloomy so much of the time took some getting used to on my part.

One bright autumn day, after soccer practice, I got home and took Charlie for his late afternoon walk. As I passed by the clearing where the stone wall was closest to the sidewalk, I felt that mysterious force pulling at me again, and I just knew that I had to go back into the woods as soon as I could. After bringing Charlie home, I jogged over to the stone wall and slowly and carefully followed its path deep into the woods, until I came to the crossed sticks I had used to mark the spot. I looked out into the distance and saw Nathaniel beckoning me. Although he was far away, I noticed that he looked different. For one thing, he was mounted on a horse. Gathering up all my courage, I stepped over the wall. The searing flash of light, the roaring in my ears, it all happened as before, but somehow I guess I knew what to expect. Although I was still afraid, I was not as terrified as I had been in the past. And Nathaniel was there, waiting for me, smiling and holding his hands out to me. To be honest with myself, I had come to think of him as my Colonial boyfriend.

Instantly, I knew why he looked different. He was no longer dressed in the shirt, vest and pants I'd seen him wearing before. Now, he wore a uniform of some sort, and I could only guess that he had joined the militia, as he'd told me he would.

"What do you think, Abigail?" he asked, as he dismounted and turned around to show me his full uniform. I took it all in as he stood in front of me and realized that he looked like those pictures of the Minuteman statue I'd seen in my history books. He was now wearing a tri-cornered hat that looked as though it was made of felt or wool, and he had what looked to be some sort of knapsack (he later told me it was called a "haversack") that was at his side, with the strap across his chest. His pants were short and cut off at the knee.

"Nathaniel," I asked, "have you really joined the militia?"

"Not just the militia, Abigail. I have been chosen to be in the Minute Company."

"What does that mean?" I asked. "In my history books I thought all of the men who fought the British here in Massachusetts were Minutemen."

"Nay, Abigail, Minutemen in our Massachusetts Bay Colony need be under thirty years of age and able-bodied. We are required to receive additional training to be ready for rapid deployment. Until this time, our militia trained but two to four times a year. But now, since the King's Intolerable Acts have incited our colony, we train three to four times a week."

"Nathaniel, this whole thing scares me. I know you want to defend the rights of your colony from the high taxes and other injustices that the King of England has demanded of the colonists, but I'm afraid if you go off to war I'll never see you again."

"Abigail, be not afraid. I have a duty to defend our colony if the situation does not improve, and I fear it will not. At this time there is talk of a boycott on English goods and in the New York colony, the inhabitants erected a gallows and hung the Lieutenant Governor in effigy. Do you not see that whatever comes to pass, my path is clear?"

"Of course I know that," I replied, feeling myself becoming emotional, "and I am proud of you for becoming a Minuteman, but I know that we may never see each other again and that makes me so sad." As I said this, I felt a tear slide down my cheek, and I realized how very much I had come to care for this man, despite the vast centuries of time separating us.

"Abigail, my heart will break to lose you again, but I must not dwell on such matters of the heart when matters at hand have become so perilous. Even now we seek to purchase gunpowder for our muskets from the Dutch to prepare for whatever Divine Providence might have in store for us."

"Should we say goodbye forever now, Nathaniel? Will we have a chance to meet again?" I asked.

"Dearest Abigail, I will try to see you again. But should this not happen, I pray that you will think of me from time to time and know that I carry you in my heart as I carry out my duty."

"Nathaniel, I will try to come to the wall as often as I can to see if you are here to meet me. If you aren't here, I'll know that you are preparing to defend our country. And everything that I've told you about our country is true. Your Minutemen fired a shot heard around the world and began a fight for independence that was the beginning of the United States of America, the greatest power the world has ever known. It started with you. I will never forget you as long as I live. You must believe me."

With that, we hugged each other as we had never done before and I kissed him with a passion that surprised me. I realized how much a part of my life this Colonial man had become, and I knew that our parting would leave a huge empty place in my life—one that I couldn't speak of to anyone. I turned and sadly walked back toward the wall. Giving a last look backward, I stepped over it and with a blinding flash and a roar, tumbled back into my own modern-day life. I stood at the wall for several minutes and watched Nathaniel as he mounted his horse and waved, riding off into the distant past.

CHAPTER 20

COPING

After that crossing, I felt a sadness I'd never experienced before. I tend to be a very upbeat person and when things get me down, I usually just tell myself that life will get better. Up to that point, the move from Las Vegas to Massachusetts had been the biggest upheaval in my life, and I thought I'd coped with it as well as most teenagers would have—maybe even better. Knowing I would probably never see Nathaniel again was so hard, because I couldn't talk about it with anyone—not my best friend, not my parents and certainly not Ethan. First of all, no one would believe me. My talk with Julie about traveling back in time certainly proved that even my closest friend would think I'd gone completely crazy. I knew I'd somehow have to cope with this on my own.

I'd lie awake at night, trying to put Nathaniel and my experience traveling back in time to meet him in perspective. "Just pretend he was your boyfriend and he broke up with you," I would tell myself. "You would just have to get over him. You only met him a few times, so it's not like you'd been going out with him forever." When I'd finally fall asleep, I would have frightening dreams that I mostly couldn't remember in the morning.

I kept pushing myself in school, harder than I ever had before. My grades by mid-quarter were in the high honor roll range, so I felt that at least I had managed to do something right. It helped to distract me and it did make me feel as though I had accomplished something important.

I guess the combination of working so hard, going to soccer practice every day and not sleeping well finally caught up with me. On a Wednesday, during the last week of September, I came home from school and it took just one look from my mom for her to jump up out of her chair.

"Abby! You look awful! Are you feeling sick?"

I dropped onto the living room couch and admitted, "Yeah, I really feel awful."

Mom helped me up to my room where I put on my PJs and crawled into my bed. She took my temperature; it was 101 degrees.

"Abby, I'm making an appointment for you to see our new doctor. I've been meaning to have you get a physical anyway, but maybe they can fit you in early tomorrow morning."

I think she was so upset because I'd always enjoyed really good health. While many of my friends missed lots of school due to colds, flu and sore throats, I'd almost never gotten sick enough to stay home from school. In fact, there were several years when I had perfect attendance. I guess this wasn't going to be one of them.

Dr. Morrow was really nice, and after she took my temperature and blood pressure, looked down my throat, and felt the glands in my neck, she did a strep test and sure enough, I had strep throat. By that time, my fever had gone up, and I was really feeling awful. On the way home we stopped at the pharmacy to pick up the prescription that Dr. Morrow had called in. I waited in the car while mom went in to get it. As soon as we got home, I went upstairs, took the antibiotic, and crawled back into bed, where I stayed for the next two days.

I did so much thinking during that time. I would doze off and then when I'd wake up, I'd think about what had taken place in the woods. Who would ever think that stepping over a stone wall could be a gateway into a long ago time? I watched some TV and drank lots of tea and ginger ale. I started realizing that I'd definitely let myself get run down by the stress of secretly meeting Nathaniel. Between schoolwork, going out with Ethan and my friends, soccer practice and just getting used to my new home, I think going back in time had just wrecked my usual good health.

It was time for a change. I started feeling better after the antibiotics began to work and as I felt better, I decided to look ahead to the future, instead of dwelling on Nathaniel and a life that was not meant to be. It seems weird to say that getting sick helped me to heal, but in a funny way, it really did.

CHAPTER 21

HOMECOMING

By October, I was completely caught up in the life of my new school. I was pushing myself academically, trying to maintain honor roll grades because I knew that junior year was the most important one for college admissions. Soccer practice took up lots of time almost every day after school. Our team was doing pretty well considering the competition. I only got to play a few times, but when I did, Coach Perez complimented me and gave me lots of encouragement.

The homecoming dance, a semi-formal, was going to be happening on the second Saturday night in October, after our home game with nearby Methuen High School. My mom and I went shopping at the Rockingham Mall for a dress for me to wear. I must have tried on at least 20 dresses before I found the perfect one. It was the most beautiful shade of blue (my mom called it "sapphire") and it had spaghetti straps and tiny sparkly stones all over the top. I had the perfect strappy sandals to wear with it too, so I didn't have to look for shoes.

Everyone at the high school was texting about who would be chosen as king and queen of homecoming. Ethan and I had been one of the couples nominated, but I didn't expect to win since I didn't know that many kids in the school who might vote for me. You weren't really allowed to have cell phones in class, but it was amazing how everyone seemed to get away with it, no matter how hard the teachers tried to figure out who was using them. Once in a while, a teacher managed to catch a kid texting and took the phone away. That meant you had to go down to the assistant principal's office after school to get it back. If it happened a second time, one of your parents would have to come in after school to meet with the assistant principal in order for you to get your phone back. I definitely was not going to be one of those kids; I just didn't take my phone out in class. It stayed in my backpack. That was so much easier than worrying about getting caught!

The day of the homecoming game was crisp and sunny, a gorgeous fall day. This really was a new experience for me, coming from the desert. By now the leaves were really colorful—reds and golds with a little bit of green left, and lots of them had already fallen on the ground where they crunched under my feet. I had read about fall—autumn—all my life and now I was actually experiencing it. Liz and I went to the game together, along with quite a few other kids. We definitely took up a big section of the bleachers. It was sort of chilly, but everyone was so excited about the game, and about the announcement of the king and queen that was to happen at halftime, that the cold didn't bother us at all. By halftime the Hillies were ahead 14-6 and the crowd was really pumped up!

Five couples had been nominated, and most of them were seniors, meaning that both members of the couple were members of the senior class. I thought for sure that Ethan and I wouldn't have much of a chance because first of all, I was a newcomer and second, I wasn't a senior. A hush fell over the bleachers as Principal Collier stepped up to the microphone.

"Good afternoon, everyone," he said as he greeted the crowd. "As you know, each year we hold an election to select the couple who will be our homecoming king and queen. They will reign over the homecoming dance tonight, and each will receive a $100 gift card that can be used at any of our local merchants."

By now the crowd had started getting noisy again, and Principal Collier had to ask them to quiet down before he could continue.

"It gives me great pleasure to announce that this year's king and queen, as voted by the overwhelming majority of the student body, are Ethan Adams, our football captain, and Abby Whittier, a member of our junior class who transferred to Haverhill High School this year from Las Vegas."

To say I was stunned would be an understatement. I just sat in my seat, unmoving and speechless, until Liz grabbed me by both shoulders and shook me.

"Abby, you have to get down there! Didn't you hear him? You're the homecoming queen! You and Ethan are the king and queen! Come on, get up and go down there!"

I don't normally consider myself to be a shy person, but then again, I've never been put in a position like that before. I got up from my bleacher seat and felt the eyes of everyone in the stands on me as I made my way down to the football field.

"OMG," I thought to myself, "please don't let me trip and fall." And then I looked down at the field and saw Ethan waiting for me and I felt so much better. Confidence flowed through me, and I could feel a big smile starting to form on my face.

It seemed as though it took forever for me to make it down to the podium where Principal Collier placed a tiara on my head and Ethan gave me a big bear hug and a kiss. Then a shiny red convertible drove onto the field and Ethan and I were helped onto the back of it so we could be driven around the field and wave to the fans. I can't even explain how I felt. It was such an amazing experience! After we arrived back at the podium, Ethan kissed me again and had to run back into the locker room to get ready to play the second half of the game. I made my way back up the bleachers to where I had been sitting before, and everyone congratulated me.

Liz, especially, was so happy she just hugged me and whispered, "See, Abby, lots of people like you, even though you're new. And it's not just because you're going out with Ethan. People think you're a nice person, just like I do."

The Hillies won the game 21-13 and I went home to get ready for the dance. My parents were both home and were as thrilled as I was about my election as homecoming queen.

"Oh, Abby, we knew you would do well here in Massachusetts," my mom said, and I could swear I saw tears in her eyes.

My dad was really proud, too, and when I got all ready for the dance in my new dress, he took a picture of me, standing on the staircase of our home, wearing my tiara. "You know you've always been my princess," he said, beaming, and I felt that I'd made both my parents really proud that day.

Ethan arrived to pick me up at 7:30, with a corsage for my wrist. He walked in and just stared at me for what seemed like a whole minute, smiling as he looked at me all dressed up.

"Wow, Abby, you look awesome, like a movie star!"

That definitely made me laugh! Apparently he had asked my Mom what color dress I was wearing because the corsage he bought looked perfect with my dress. Ethan was looking pretty good himself, in a blue blazer that matched his eyes and a shirt and tie in different shades of blue. It was the first time I'd ever seen him in anything but jeans and a casual shirt.

The dance was so much fun! We danced most of the time, except for about a half hour when we had to sit on fake thrones and reign over the dance with the other members of our "court," who were the other couples who'd been nominated for king and queen. It was corny, but fun. All in all, it was a night I won't forget for many years to come.

CHAPTER 22

GIVING IN

I really thought I had completely conquered my desire to see Nathaniel again, but the pull of that stone wall was way more powerful than I had admitted to myself. Each time I walked past it, I could feel myself wanting to follow it into the woods. I kept ignoring the feeling, until one day I just gave in.

By now it was the beginning of November. The trees were pretty bare and it was cold out. I could see my breath when I went out in the morning. My mom had taken me shopping to buy a warm parka, a matching hat, scarf and gloves, and snow boots. I had even started wearing shearling-lined boots to school. I'd never really experienced winter before, so I was getting excited to see a real snowfall for the first time. It's not that I'd never seen snow. Once in a blue moon it would snow in Las Vegas, but it wouldn't last more than a few hours. Schools would be called off, and by noon, it would all have melted and evaporated, leaving no trace. I was also looking forward to the holidays in New England, hoping for a white Christmas. I could send pictures to my friends to show them how a real Christmas should look.

Late one afternoon, after soccer season had ended, I decided I just had to try and see if Nathaniel was waiting for me at the wall. I grabbed my flashlight and jogged over to the clearing where I made my way through the underbrush. It was easier this time of year because most of the leaves and vines had died off so I could see my way more clearly. When I got to the Crossing Place (that's what I'd named it) I looked over the wall, into the distance, and he was there! Nathaniel was waiting for me, on his horse, and beckoning me to cross over. After more than a month of not experiencing the travel back in time, stepping over the wall was almost as terrifying as it had been the first time. The noise, the flash of intense bright light, and the feeling that I was tumbling down an endless tunnel really scared me to death! Then I was standing there, dressed in the same Colonial outfit, and Nathaniel was dismounting from his horse to give me a loving kiss.

"Dearest Abigail, how I have missed you," he began. "I have been off training with the militia and minutemen, but so often my thoughts have been of you. 'Tis terribly hard to put you out of mind."

"Nathaniel, I've often thought about you, too, and I've hoped that you didn't get hurt in any battles with the British," I replied, as he held me closer.

"Nay, we have been preparing for the worst, but to this date, we have had nought to fight. I fear the worst is to come, though, and I had hoped to see you one last time before I travel to Boston."

"Somehow I knew that," I answered. "I don't know how I knew, but each time I would walk past the stone wall, I would feel that you were calling to me through the years. It sounds impossible, but that's how I felt. I knew I had to come here today. Why do you have to go to Boston? What's happening there?"

Nathaniel explained that beginning in 1768, British troops had been stationed in Boston to protect the officials appointed by the King of England who were there to enforce the King's unpopular laws. Things between the colonists and the British troops had gotten very tense.

"And so you must go to Boston to help out if any fight happens between these British troops and the people of Boston?"

"Yea, that is what I am bound to do, Abigail. My colony is in danger and the time has arrived to stand up to the violation of our rights by the King."

"Nathaniel, I'll pray for your safe return. If we don't meet again, I'll never forget you or what you sacrificed for our country. I only wish you could see what Massachusetts has become in our time. You've come to mean so much to me. I must believe that God has a reason why we were brought together, since it's obvious to me that our lives can't be joined beyond these few brief meetings."

"Abigail, I will carry my memories of you in my heart as I go to whatever destiny has in store for me. I cannot understand this travel through time, nor can I imagine the life you have explained to me. I have only the memory of you now, and that is what is dearest to me. I also will pray that the Almighty will grant you a long and happy life, even though you say it cannot be with me."

And with that last heartfelt speech, we hugged once more and without looking back, Nathaniel mounted his horse and watched as I crossed back over the wall, back to the present, to the country he helped create.

CHAPTER 23

WINTER ARRIVES

Thanksgiving in Massachusetts! I have to admit that it was a really different experience to celebrate the holiday in the state where it began, instead of in Las Vegas. My parents were so happy to be in their home state, and I could tell how excited mom was to be cooking a traditional turkey dinner in our beautiful new kitchen. They had invited three other couples to have dinner with us, people they had met through my dad's work, so my mom had bought a 23-pound turkey to be sure there would be plenty for everyone.

I was going to the Thanksgiving Day football game with Liz and some other friends before coming home for dinner, but I helped my mom the night before—getting all of the silverware, dishes, plates and glasses out and helping her open the dining room table to its full length. When I got home after the game, I peeled potatoes and squash, set the table, and did a few other things to help her get ready for our guests. The house looked really beautiful, with a fire in the living room fireplace, candles on the mantle, and a gorgeous centerpiece in the middle of the table.

As people arrived, I took their coats and brought them upstairs, while my dad mixed drinks for them. Everyone commented on how beautiful the house looked, and I realized that even though it wasn't a glamorous home like the one we had lived in back in Las Vegas, it was really much more "homey." It felt like home to me now, and it was hard for me to believe I'd lived here less than six months.

Just when we sat down to eat, I glanced out the window and jumped up, "Snow!" I cried, as I ran to the window.

"Abby, we forget you haven't seen snow more than a couple of times in your life," my dad said laughing. "Come sit down and eat. I don't think it will be melting any time soon."

The meal was so delicious! (I had probably forgotten to mention that my mom is a great cook.) After helping to clear the table, I put on my boots, parka, gloves and scarf and ran out to walk in the snow with Charlie who seemed to enjoy running around in it with his little nose plowing up the snow as he ran along. It was the perfect Thanksgiving Day!

By late afternoon, the snow was at least seven inches deep, and I realized that even if Nathaniel were at the wall, I wouldn't be able to push my way through the woods when there was any large amount of snow piled up. I didn't have boots high enough, and I doubted that the wall would even be visible.

Back at home, after all the guests had left, I asked, "How long does winter last here?"

"That depends," my mom answered. "It can last until April, if it's a bad winter, and since it snowed so much and it's just the end of November, I have a feeling that this may be one of those winters where the ground is covered in snow from November until spring."

I thought about this and hoped there would be a thaw sometime before April so I could at least try to get back to the Crossing Place, but I was resigned to the fact that Nathaniel and I had said our goodbyes and that he had gone to serve his country. I needed to look to the future now.

CHAPTER 24

FUTURE PLANS

By Christmas vacation, Ethan had already heard from his first-choice college. He had decided to apply Early Decision to Tufts University in Medford, Massachusetts, because the football coach had urged him to consider playing for the Jumbos, and he liked the idea of living in a dorm but being close enough to come home whenever he felt like it. I had visited the campus with him, and I really liked it too. Since I was only a junior, I had just gotten my PSAT scores back and I was thrilled that they were so high!

"Abby, you should think about applying to Tufts next year too," Ethan urged, "then we could continue seeing each other in college."

"Ethan, I'd really planned to apply to college back in Las Vegas when I moved out here," I replied, "but I'm liking New England more and more the longer I live here, so I'll definitely think about colleges around here."

"Abs, you are so smart! I just know you'll get accepted wherever you apply, so I hope you'll apply to Tufts, or at least to schools close by. I'll really miss seeing you every day."

"I'll miss you too, Ethan, but I have to check out lots of colleges and apply where I think I'll fit in the best."

I was really happy with my grades and so were my parents. I'd made high honor roll for the first quarter and was keeping my grades up second quarter too. After Christmas vacation, there were just two weeks before midterm exams. I planned to study really hard so I could make high honor roll for the semester.

But now it was Christmas vacation, and I was completely thrilled that Julie would be flying in the day after Christmas. It was all I could think about. I had bought and wrapped my presents for mom and dad and for Ethan and Liz, but I still had to figure out what to get for Julie. I finally decided that since Nevada had no major league teams, I'd buy Julie a Red Sox hoodie and an official Sox cap to wear back home. I knew she'd like that.

Christmas morning dawned and it was snowing a light, fluffy snow. I put my parka over my PJs, jumped into my boots and ran outside to take a photo of my house with my iPhone to send to everyone back in Las Vegas. It really was the perfect Christmas photo, and the house—with evergreen trees coated in snow, lights sparkling all around it, and a Christmas tree in the front window—looked like a movie set. My parents and I opened our gifts, and I was happy that they loved what I got them. I'd gone back to the Buttonwoods Museum and bought a History of Haverhill for my dad, and I'd bought a genealogy book about the Dustin Family for my mom. I'd also bought them a bunch of stocking stuffers and a gift card for dinner at Olivia's, one of their favorite local restaurants.

My gifts were mostly clothes, picked out by my mom, who knew exactly what I needed and what would look good on me. She was so fashion-conscious that everything she bought fit me perfectly, and I just loved all of it! But the biggest surprise of all was yet to come.

"Abby, did you happen to look in the garage?" my dad asked.

"Dad, why would I do that?"

"Well I really think you should," he answered with a laugh.

So I ran over to the door that led into the garage and threw it open. There, parked in the third garage space, was the most amazing gift I could ever have hoped for: a brand new, bright red Toyota RAV4!

"Mom, Dad, is this really for me? Is this my car? I can't believe you'd actually buy me a car for Christmas!" I knew I was babbling, but I was completely shocked!

"Abby, we know you'll be getting your learner's permit soon, and we wanted you to learn to drive in a car that has all-wheel-drive and is as safe as it can possibly be. Driving in New England, with snow and ice, isn't like driving in Las Vegas, so we thought you should have a car that was meant for roads like these."

I just couldn't believe my eyes as I sat in this awesome car with its tan leather interior and amazing new car smell!

"I can't tell you how thankful I am," I began.

"We know how hard the move was for you, Honey," my mom interrupted, "and we're just so happy you've adapted as well as you have and are doing well here in Haverhill."

"I actually love living here," I told them. And then the three of us just hugged, and I think we all felt grateful for everything we had as a family. I was really overwhelmed by their gift of a new car. Now I couldn't wait to turn 16 and get my learner's permit.

Later that day, Ethan and Liz came over and we exchanged gifts. I had ordered a Tufts sweatshirt and sweatpants for Ethan, and a Tufts tank top and shorts for Liz. They both loved the gifts.

"Abby, when did you manage to get these?" Ethan asked.

"I had to order them online," I told him. "I had no way to get back to the Tufts campus—remember? I don't have my license yet!"

Ethan gave me a beautiful gold necklace with my initial, A, and a garnet, my birthstone. He told me he had picked it out himself, but if I wanted to exchange it, I could.

"Are you kidding?" I asked, "I love it!" And I quickly put it around my neck.

Liz got me a really awesome keychain with the Boston Red Sox logo for my car key when I got my license. She knew I couldn't wait until the end of January when I'd turn 16 and could take driver's ed and get my permit. When I showed them my new car, both of them ran over and sat in it, and we all talked about how much fun we'd have driving it to the beach next summer.

"This car is just amazing, Abby," breathed Liz. "Your parents are just incredible!"

"I am really, really lucky," I replied, and I knew this was so true.

We picked Julie up at Logan Airport on Dec. 26. We actually cried, we were so happy to see each other again, and we hugged so hard and so long that my dad finally had to break it up saying, "Okay, girls, we really have to get going to beat the rush-hour traffic!"

On the way home, I pointed out different places I knew, like the Bunker Hill Monument, and the glass tower at the Prudential Center, but Julie's biggest thrill was seeing the Atlantic Ocean.

"Abby, I can't believe I'm actually here, in Massachusetts, and there's the ocean, right there!"

"Julie, you're on the East Coast. Of course the ocean is right there!"

"I know, but it's just so amazing! I can't believe you live here."

When we got to my house, Julie just sat still and stared. "Abby, it's so all-American looking. I mean it looks like those houses that they lived in back in Colonial times."

"Come on, Julie, it may look like those houses, but that's because most of the homes here in Massachusetts are built like the ones they built back then. Come inside so you can bring your stuff upstairs and we can have a snack or something. You must be starving!"

We had so much fun together it was like we'd never been apart. I took her over to the high school to see it and introduced her to Ethan and Liz. She met some of my other friends too. Ethan and I drove her into Boston twice, and we walked around Faneuil Hall Marketplace. I made her eat a plate of fried clams and she loved them. We lucked out as far as the weather went, so we went on a Freedom Trail Walk and saw many of the famous Boston landmarks like the Boston Common. We also walked through the Granary Burial Ground on Tremont Street, dating back to the 1600s, where Samuel Adams, John Hancock and Paul Revere are buried. One of the most interesting places was the Old South Meeting House at the corner of Milk and Washington Streets where 5,000 colonists met and organized the Boston Tea Party in 1773.

"Abby, I feel as though I just took a walk back in time," Julie told me that night. "I understand now why you asked me that time on the phone if I believed in time travel. Every place around here has so much history. It's not at all like living out West in Las Vegas. Las Vegas has only been around for about 150 years."

"I know. There were colonists here since way before the Revolutionary War. People were living in Massachusetts since the 1600s."

Most of the time she was here, Julie and I spent talking. We talked about my friends back at Palm Desert High, about my new friends here in Haverhill and about our plans after high school. I told her I was thinking of applying to colleges here in New England.

"Abby! I thought you were coming back to Nevada for college," she cried, and I thought she really was going to burst into tears. "Is it because of Ethan? I mean he's hot and all, but you can't change your life just because of him."

"No, Jules, I really like it here. I like the seasons and I like being near the ocean. I guess I'm glad I got to experience living in another part of the country. You never know what you're missing until you try something new. Why don't you think about applying to colleges out here?"

I could see Julie thinking seriously about this before she answered.

"You know, I just might. It sort of appeals to me to go to college someplace different. Maybe next summer I'll come back out here, if my parents will let me, and look at some colleges around Boston. My grades and test scores aren't as good as yours though."

"Not to worry, Jules, there are so many colleges around Boston, and you have good grades. You usually make the honor roll, right? I know you'd get accepted at lots of them if you applied."

When we took Julie to the airport on Dec. 30, both of us cried when we had to say goodbye. I knew I'd really miss her all over again. She promised to talk to her parents about coming back in the summer to look at Boston colleges. That made her leaving a little bit easier.

Ethan and I had decided to go out to an early dinner at a really nice restaurant on New Year's Eve before going to a house party. I think he knew I felt sad because Julie had left, so he tried to raise my spirits throughout the night. At midnight we toasted each other with champagne that someone had managed to buy, and after a long, long kiss, Ethan looked into my eyes and declared, "I think I really love you, Abby Whittier."

I was sort of shocked to hear him say those words, and I wasn't really ready to say them back, so I just smiled and answered, "Ethan Adams, I think that's the champagne talking!" He hugged me and we left it like that.

CHAPTER 25

A BLANKET OF SNOW

My birthday arrived, and my dad took me down to the Registry of Motor Vehicles to get my learner's permit. I was already signed up for drivers' ed after school, and I was so excited to think that in a few months, I would be driving around in my new car! Of course, there were some pretty stiff laws in Massachusetts for young drivers, but I was sure they wouldn't be a problem for me. I'd always been someone who obeyed the laws; I'd never been a rebel, and I wasn't going to start now. Driving was something I was going to take very seriously. There were times when friends had tried to get me to cheat or break a rule. I never condemned them for what they did or stopped being their friend. I just felt better following my own heart and not having to worry about getting caught. I actually think my friends respected me for that.

As my mom had predicted, the ground had been covered in snow since that Thanksgiving Day snowstorm. It seemed to snow at least once a week, and we had snow days off from school for many of them. I got used to listening to the weather reports on the 6 p.m. news. If snow was predicted, I'd immediately turn on the TV in my room when I woke up to see if Haverhill was on the list of school closings. It actually had to snow pretty hard for our city to close its schools. Mostly they had delayed openings and made each class a few minutes shorter, instead of closing school completely. I still took Charlie on his afternoon walk each day after I got home from school. I'd gotten involved in a few after-school clubs that winter, so it was almost dark when I'd take him for his walk. I'd bought him a really cute red and white striped sweater for Christmas and would put it on him before taking him outdoors. I'm not saying he liked it, but I do think it kept his little body warmer, and he looked so adorable in it!

One day, as we passed by the stone wall, I felt that pull again—the pull to go to the Crossing Place. I had my snow boots on and was dressed warmly, so I picked Charlie up and walked into the clearing, intending to see if I could get through the naked branches and brambles far enough to make the crossing, but the snow was way too deep. By the time I'd walked beyond the clearing, the snow was at least six inches over the tops of my boots, and I could see that it got even deeper as it went further into the woods, where the sun almost never reached the ground. I realized that even if Nathaniel was waiting for me, there would have to be lots of melting before I could possibly make my way over to see him again. That thought saddened me, but I knew that he'd understand if I didn't come.

It's strange that I'd never been the least bit interested in history before moving to Massachusetts, but now I read everything I could get my hands on, along with tons of articles online, about the events leading up to the American Revolution. Maybe I was hoping to see a mention of Nathaniel's name somewhere. It definitely helped me in my AP U.S. History class. I wrote my research paper on the Minutemen and got one of the best grades in the class. How could anyone have known that I had actually met one of them? No one would have believed me anyway.

CHAPTER 26

A LONG WINTER

January turned into February, and the snow just kept coming down. I honestly couldn't believe how much snow we got, but everyone else just seemed to take it for granted. My parents had hired a company to plow our driveway early in the morning because my dad had to get into work unless the City of Boston was shut down. They actually did that sometimes when the snowstorms got too dangerous. The mayor would go on TV and ask companies to keep people from coming into work so that plows could clear the streets. I had never heard of anything like that before.

On snow days when school was called off, Ethan usually came over, either in his car if he could get around, or on his cross-country skis if the roads weren't plowed. He lent me a pair of Liz's old cross-country skis and taught me how to use them. We had so much fun skiing on the golf course! As long as I dressed in layers, I didn't even get very cold. After we'd had enough of the outdoors, we'd go back to my house and drink some hot chocolate in front of the fireplace. I started really loving those snow days! I passed my written driver's test, but I decided that I'd wait until there was a little less snow and ice on the roads before I started actually going out to take driving lessons. I was so afraid of getting in an accident in my new car.

By March, the worst of the snow had melted, so my mom took me out driving on the streets in our development. Northwoods only had about a hundred homes, so there was never much traffic on our streets. I was also taking lessons from a local driving school, so I was learning fast. By the time March ended, I was feeling pretty confident at the wheel, but I'd have to wait for a few months to take the driving test, and that was fine with me. I wanted to pass it on the first try.

School was still really hard. I spent hours on homework each night and was also taking an SAT prep course to get ready to take the test at the beginning of May. I can't say I was looking forward to that, but I knew that a lot depended on my SAT scores. I was doing well on the practice tests, but I needed to work on some of the math sections because I'd always been better at English than math.

Ethan was starting to look forward to graduation at the beginning of June. He'd already asked me to the senior prom, and of course I'd said yes. I knew I'd need another prom dress, and I hated to ask my mom to buy me another one, but she seemed perfectly happy to go shopping with me again. This time, I thought I'd like a long dress. We started shopping in early April, and each Saturday, we'd head out to a mall, I'd try on a few dresses and then we'd go out to lunch. It was really the first time since our move that I'd spent "together time" with my mom. It always seemed that one of us was busy doing something, so this was a chance for us to enjoy shopping together and not feel rushed. I finally found the prom dress I wanted at Macy's and I really loved it! It was white chiffon and had only one shoulder strap. There were bursts of rhinestones on the top and the neckline was asymmetrical. I thought it was really stunning, and mom was going to lend me jewelry and other accessories to match so I didn't need to go out and buy a bag or shoes.

It had thawed enough that I could walk Charlie on the sidewalks of Northwoods, and I could tell how much he was enjoying getting back to his old routine. It almost seemed like spring in April, but there were a few more snow flurries that let me know winter was still around. Since there had been so much melting, I decided I had to try to get to the Crossing Place, and late one afternoon, I tucked my jeans into my boots and tried to get there. I managed to push the brambles and branches out of the way and amazingly, my marker had managed to stay in place during all of the snow we had. But there was no sign of Nathaniel on the other side of the wall. I went back several other times to see if he'd appear to me, but he never did. As sad as this made me, I had already accepted the fact a while ago that I'd probably not see him again, and so I finally stopped going to the stone wall. I no longer felt that strange attraction when I walked past it and that, in itself, told me that Nathaniel was not there waiting for me.

CHAPTER 27

FINALLY...SPRING!

I was beginning to think that spring would never come. As much as I liked my new home and living in Massachusetts, the long, cold, snowy winter sort of made me homesick for Las Vegas. The slushy sidewalks and giant potholes in the streets were really dangerous to walk on. Sometimes, you didn't even see the holes until you were actually on top of them, and I have to admit, I took a few falls walking Charlie around the neighborhood. Then, halfway through April, I started to see signs that spring was finally coming. My mom had planted lots of bulbs around our front walk, and one day, some crocuses magically appeared! I started seeing buds on some of our trees, and in the early evening, I could hear sounds in the woods in back of our house. My dad said the sounds were made by tiny frogs called "spring peepers." It was obvious that things were coming back to life.

Ethan was pitching for the Hillies' baseball team, so I tried to go to as many of their home games as I could. He was doing really well, and as the days got warmer, Liz and I and a bunch of other kids would really look forward to hanging out in the bleachers after school to watch the games. I was so proud of Ethan! He had really managed to do it all, and hadn't even seemed to be trying, although I knew he had worked hard to achieve his goals. He'd been captain of the football team and helped them to a winning season, achieved high grades and gotten into the college of his choice, and now he was doing a great job for the baseball team. It was hard to believe that we'd been together since last summer. I knew that my life would not have been half as much fun, and that I probably would not have enjoyed my move to Massachusetts, if it hadn't been for him. The seniors would be graduating at the beginning of

June, but we, the underclassmen, would be in school until almost the end of June because of all the snow days that we had to make up. When Julie and I went on FaceTime, she couldn't believe how long we were in school.

"Abby, we're out at the end of May, for God's sake," she yelled. "I absolutely cannot believe you have to go to school until almost July!"

"Jules, by the end of June it will probably be over 100 degrees in Las Vegas," I replied, laughing, "and we'll just be starting summer out here! At least I won't suffocate when it gets to 113 degrees out there like I used to!"

We started making plans for Julie to come and visit colleges in Massachusetts. She'd actually managed to talk her parents into letting her apply to some schools here, and her excitement over going to college in Boston was really contagious.

"Abs, you are so lucky you live in a place where there are literally hundreds of colleges. Boston is definitely **the** place for college in America!"

"I know, Jules, and if I don't get into Tufts, I'll apply to lots of other places. I know I want to stay here now and my parents are completely over the moon about it. I think they were really afraid I'd end up wanting to go back to Vegas to attend UNLV."

I have to admit, life was going along pretty smoothly for me. I remembered back to the year before, in April, when I'd found out that I had to leave Las Vegas and move to Massachusetts. I wouldn't have believed that I would learn to like living on the East Coast, have really awesome new friends—not to mention an amazing boyfriend—and even want to stay here for college. I guess it shows that you have to give new things a try before you make up your mind about whether you like them or not. Right?

And yet, as I studied hard to keep up my grades and went out with Ethan, Liz and my other new friends, in the back of my mind I would think of Nathaniel and my strange travels back in time. He was such a brave man and loved his Abigail so much, even though I knew that I wasn't, couldn't have been, that girl. He believed I was and he had wanted to marry me. It was really weird to imagine what life must have been like for girls my age back in Colonial times. Instead of going to high school, playing sports, going to proms and planning for college, they married young, had lots of children and probably died before they even had a chance to enjoy life. Every day, as I passed by the stone wall, my mind went back to the times that I'd stepped over it. Sometimes I thought my mind had been playing tricks on me, but then I'd go into my jewelry box and find the note and the button that I'd hidden underneath the lining, and I'd know that it had really happened. I realized that life had to go on, and I tried to put the whole experience in a separate corner of my mind and live in the here and now.

My dad took me for my drivers' road test at the beginning of May, and I passed with flying colors! I was so proud of myself! The parallel parking part was what had worried me the most, but when it came time for that, I managed to do it perfectly, as if I'd been doing it all my life. I was now a licensed Massachusetts driver. Of course, I had to be sure to follow all those restrictions on young drivers because I'd never, ever want to get my license suspended for breaking some minor rule. I had that gorgeous little RAV4 waiting for me in our garage, and I couldn't wait to get behind the wheel!

CHAPTER 28

HEARTBREAK

T he school year was winding down by the end of May, and we were mostly reviewing in every class, getting ready for the final exams that counted for 20 percent of our final grade. I was determined to ace them all. Ethan and I had been talking a lot about Tufts admissions, and I knew my best chance of getting in would be to finish the year with top grades. Tufts had gotten more and more selective, and they took only the top students from our high school.

Our AP U.S. History teacher, Mrs. Case, decided that we should visit the Haverhill Historical Society and the Old Pentucket Burial Ground as a "capstone experience" to end our year. I was excited to go back to the museum to tour the houses there, because when I went there the first time, I only looked at the exhibits and didn't have time for a guided tour. It was so funny how I'd fallen in love with the history of Colonial times and of New England, in general. Somehow, moving here had made me wake up to what history was all about. It wasn't just dates and wars. It was about real people. I guess my travels back in time had made all of this meaningful to me in a way that no history book ever could have. But, of course, no one could know about that.

On a beautiful spring day, just after Memorial Day weekend, our history class piled on a bus and went over to The Buttonwoods. The tour guide was amazing. She took us through all three buildings on the property: the Duncan White home that was an example of a federalist Colonial; the John Ward house that was the home of a tenant farmer; and the Daniel Hunkins shoe shop where a shoemaker had made shoes by hand. I found out that Haverhill had been known as the "Queen Slipper City" because of the beautiful shoes that had been made here, and the museum had many examples of those slippers.

One of the things that was really cool was the Worshipping Tree that stood in front of the Duncan White house. We were told that it was about 350 years old and was the place where early settlers in the Haverhill area had come to worship on the Sabbath, before any church had been built. It made me wonder if Nathaniel had stood here, under this very oak tree, to pray. Then I realized that when I had met him, it was about the time of the American Revolution, so I guess by then they'd probably have built an actual church.

After the tour, we all walked down to the Pentucket Burial Ground, around the corner from the museum. It was an eerie feeling, standing among those ancient graves. Our guide pointed out the grave of one of the judges who had presided over the Salem Witch Trials, but had resigned in protest. It was good to know that not everyone had been caught up in the hysteria of those trials where women could be hanged just because a neighbor pointed a finger at them and accused them of being a witch.

We wandered around the cemetery, looking at the headstones, many of them crumbling from age. I thought it was sad that they weren't preserved better. You could hardly read the inscriptions on some of them. Then, as I walked to the part of the burial ground that was furthest from the street, I was drawn to one gravestone that had a small American flag, waving in the breeze, firmly planted in the ground next to it. I walked over, feeling an overwhelming sense of dread, and standing next to it I read:

Heer lies buried the body of
Major Nathaniel Prescott White
Who departed this life July 10, 1778
Age of 31 years
He served his country in the Revolution

I felt all the air leave my body and my heart was beating so loudly, I was sure everyone would hear it. My Nathaniel. He had died in the Revolution, fighting the British, to make this country, my country, possible. I felt tears start, and even though I tried hard to stop them, they ran down my face. Mrs. Case noticed me standing by myself and came over to see what I was doing.

When she saw the tears I was trying hard to hide, she exclaimed, "Abby! What's going on? Why are you upset? Is it being in a cemetery?"

"Yes, I guess so," I replied, sniffling. "Maybe it's just sad that so many of these people are forgotten and their graves are crumbling that just overwhelmed me. I'll be fine, honestly."

She handed me a tissue and I wiped away my tears, smiled at her and re-joined the rest of the class as we boarded the bus taking us back to the high school. Thank God it was the last class of the day. I walked home by myself, happy that Ethan was at baseball practice, and thought about Nathaniel and how he had given his life for his country. My feelings for him had been so real, even though I knew it had been an impossible situation. Somehow, through some strange and amazing twist of fate, I had been thrown through time to meet him. It made me so sad to think about him and how much he had cared about me.

When I got home mom was out and the house was empty, so I grabbed a bottle of water and ran up to my room. I took out the note and the button from my jewelry box and held them in my hand while I thought about the Revolutionary War hero, my hero, who lay buried in the Pentucket Burial Ground. I resolved to never forget his sacrifice as long as I lived.

CHAPTER 29

FULL CIRCLE

Although the visit to the burial ground had left me feeling sad, I knew I had to hide my true feelings from everyone. Ethan was so excited about graduation, and Liz and my other friends were looking forward to summer vacation, so I managed to put those sad feelings in the back of my mind and concentrate on studying for finals and looking forward to the senior prom. Liz was going with Josh, so it was going to be even more fun. The afternoon of the prom, we had appointments at a salon at the same time for mani-pedis and to have our hair done. One of Ethan's friends had parents who owned a boat docked at a marina up in Newburyport, and he was having an after-prom party there. I was just hoping it was going to be nice weather so we wouldn't get soaked. One thing I had definitely learned about New England was that you could never count on the weather if you were planning any outdoor activities.

Senior week arrived, and it made me really nostalgic, because I knew that next year, Ethan wouldn't be at the high school. Looking back on everything that we'd done, I realized that we'd had a really amazing year together. From the beginning when I'd met him at the pool right up through our being elected homecoming king and queen, and then through the holidays and into the spring, he'd really made my life so much fun, and I knew I'd miss him when he went away to college.

Liz and I went to our salon appointments, and although she decided to wear her hair up for the prom, I decided that I wanted to just leave mine down. I always felt better about myself when my hair was long. She did try to convince me, though, and I almost gave in.

"Come on, Abby, try it for once. I know you'd look beautiful if you wore your hair up. Then you could see those sparkly crystal earrings better."

"Sorry, Liz, I have thought about it and I think I like it just the way it is. I know Ethan likes it down too, so that's another reason to wear it long."

We went home to get dressed, and when I put on my prom dress and looked in the mirror, I felt amazing! It was the first time I had ever worn a full-length dress, and it made me feel like a princess in a fairy tale! My mom just stood there looking at me, as though she couldn't believe her eyes, and my dad took a deep breath in as I walked down the stairs.

"Abigail, you look so absolutely stunning," was all he could say.

I felt wonderful and was so happy I had picked this dress for the prom. When Ethan arrived, he also seemed speechless when he saw me. He'd brought me a corsage of tiny white roses that was just perfect, and he pinned them, with mom's help, on the strap of my gown. I really felt elegant! Ethan looked incredible in his white tux and blue shirt. His blue eyes seemed bluer than usual, and my parents took so many photos of us that we finally had to stop them because the limo that was waiting outside still had to stop and pick up Josh and Liz. Besides, I told them that we'd have a formal photo taken at the prom and I'd be sure to order an extra one for them.

The prom was held at Winnekenni Castle, right in Haverhill on Kenoza Lake. Some kids in the senior class wanted it to be held at a Boston hotel, but when the class treasurer looked into the cost of renting a ballroom in Boston and compared it with having the prom at our own castle, it was so much less expensive that there really was no contest. The money the class saved was going to be used to help pay for a really special yearbook, so everyone was going to benefit—at least that was Ethan's opinion. I had to agree with him, because not everyone was going to the prom, but everyone would probably want to buy a yearbook. So if saving money on the prom rental would make the cost of the yearbook more affordable, then it seemed like a good idea to me, too.

When the four of us got to the castle, we were so blown away by how gorgeous it looked. I'd seen it in the daytime when we'd gone to some events like the Chowda Festival and the Haunted House, but to see it all lit up and decorated for the prom was a sight I won't soon forget. It was really like a magical castle out of a fairy tale, and we were the princes and princesses! I was so dazzled by it that I almost tripped getting out of the limo, probably because I wasn't used to wearing such a long dress with heels. But luckily Ethan caught me and kept me from falling, so I didn't ruin my dress or my dignity.

We had so much fun dancing to the DJ all night. The dinner was really great too. The class had decided on a sit-down dinner, instead of a buffet, and I thought it was a lot nicer to be served, instead of having to go through a line and hoping I wouldn't spill anything on my dress. Everyone said my dress was gorgeous, so I was really happy that mom and I had picked it out and that I had decided on something more formal. Lots of the girls wore really short skirts, but a few, like me, had decided on the more formal look, and it seemed to go with having the prom in the castle.

After the prom, we drove up to Newburyport and partied on Ethan's friend's boat—or should I call it a yacht? It was really a pretty big boat and had lots of room for all of us who'd been invited. Ethan's friend Ron showed everyone around, pointed out where the bathroom, called the "head," was and explained how to use it. There were tons of munchies, and I knew lots of the kids there had brought booze, but Ethan and I played it safe and just drank ginger ale. We'd be driving home in the early hours of the morning, and the last thing we'd want would be to get stopped for DUI, or worse yet, to get in an accident because Ethan had been drinking. Both of us had way too much to lose.

We finally left at about 3 a.m. and started the drive back to Haverhill. Ethan had taken his parents' car up to Newburyport after the limo had dropped us back at his house, so it was just the two of us on the ride back from the after-prom party. I was so exhausted that I could barely keep my eyes open, but Ethan seemed wide awake.

"Abby, I really need to ask you something," he began, and I immediately came to full attention.

"What's wrong, Ethan? Didn't you have a good time? I thought we had the best time ever!"

"It's not that. It's just that for the past couple of weeks, I've felt that you've been different, sort of sad even. Is there something you're not telling me? I feel as though I know you so well, but it's like you're hiding something from me."

And so, as we drove into Haverhill, I opened up to him as much as I could.

"Ethan, I think it started when our AP History class visited the Pentucket Burial Ground. I just stood there and it made me so sad to see all of those graves, some of them hundreds of years old, and most of them crumbling, and you could barely read the inscriptions on the gravestones. It just made me realize how short life is, and also how many people lived and died here before us. I guess I never saw so much history back in Las Vegas."

As we entered Haverhill center, I pointed out the statue of Hannah Duston and explained to Ethan, "I never mentioned this, but one of the reasons my mother wanted to come back to Massachusetts is because we're descended from Hannah Duston. My mother's maiden name and my middle name are Duston. I never knew the story until we moved here and my mom showed me the statue. Somehow it made me feel more connected with this place, with this city."

Ethan pulled over to the curb and took my hands in his. He looked at me with his piercing blue eyes and replied, "Abigail Whittier, I never told you this before, but since you've been to the Pentucket Burial Ground, you may have noticed that there's one very old gravestone that has a small American flag next to it. My family tends that stone and makes sure that there's always a flag next to it. Nathaniel Prescott White was an ancestor of mine. My middle name is Prescott. I'm Ethan Prescott Adams. It really is strange that we both should have ancestors who lived in the same city, don't you think?"

And then I knew. As ridiculous as it may sound to some people, I knew that we were meant to be together. I knew that my parents were meant to move back to Massachusetts, to Haverhill, and to a place where I would find my true soul mate. I realized why, from that very first FaceTime conversation with Ethan, I'd felt as though I'd known him all my life. He was the living, breathing incarnation of Nathaniel White that Abigail Whittier had loved so many centuries ago.

"Thank you for telling me that," I whispered, "I somehow feel as though we were meant to be together. I was so upset when my parents told me we were moving to Massachusetts, but now I believe that fate brought us together. Can you possibly believe that?"

"Abby, I've **always** thought we were meant to be together, from the first moment I saw you at the pool. There's never been any doubt in my mind that someday, after we finished college, we'd marry and have a family together. It's what I'd always hoped you'd say. But I know you're younger than me and you don't have to make that commitment now."

"No, Ethan, I want to. I pledge to you that I will always be your Abby. I won't change my mind. We'll be together from now until forever, just like it was meant to be."

EPILOGUE

That's where my strange journey ends. Ethan and I did stay together. We're both at Tufts now, enjoying college life. For Christmas in my freshman year, Ethan proposed and gave me his grandmother's diamond ring that had been in his family for generations. I think my parents were surprised, and maybe a little bit worried, that we had made our commitment to each other before really going out with lots of other people, but we convinced them and Ethan's parents that we were completely sure of our love for each other.

You're probably wondering whether I'll ever tell Ethan about crossing over the stone wall and traveling back in time to meet Nathaniel. Sometimes I still go to my jewelry box and take out the note and button, hold them in my hand, and think about Nathaniel. I try to decide whether I should explain my trip back in time to the man I'm going to marry. Then I put those things away and tell myself that he wouldn't believe me, even if I showed him the note and button as proof. I think I'll have to keep this secret for the rest of my life, but each time he visits the Pentucket Burial Ground to tend the grave of Nathaniel Prescott White, I'll go with him and help keep the memory of that brave American hero alive in my heart.

END

ACKNOWLEDGMENTS

To my friends and neighbors who encouraged me to continue writing, I offer my sincerest thanks. Special thanks to my husband, Jack, for his unwavering support; to my son, Eric, for his grammatical prowess; to Taylor Gischel, who educated me in the speech and attitudes of her generation of teens; and to Kendall Holmes Lavallee, who graciously allowed me to photograph her in front of the stone wall. The two guidance counselors appearing in this book are composites of the caring and compassionate colleagues I had the good fortune to work beside during my 30-year career in that profession. Every school day, they offer comfort to students experiencing life crises. Finally, I must pay tribute to my adopted hometown of Haverhill, Massachusetts—a city with a long and vibrant history, currently undergoing a renaissance. Living here has inspired me to write.